At the Wallingham Theatre Club, an American play was in rehearsal. Several baseball bats were in use as props. And it was a baseball bat that had been used to murder Raymond Denton – the weapon had been found on the common, tossed into a trench. According to the voluble Mrs McNaughton, around three hundred and five members of the club knew of the existence of the bats . . . and had access to them. Oddly enough, Sarah Mellison, one of the club's leading lights, had been seen only the previous night fooling around with the clubs . . . more oddly still, she had been the first to discover the body of the unfortunate Denton . . .

Also by John Creasey

FIND THE BODY
FIRST A MURDER
RUN AWAY TO MURDER
DON'T LET HIM KILL
THE BLACK SPIDERS
THE LONG SEARCH
DEATH IN THE TREES
THE CRIMEHATERS
DEATH IN A HURRY
DAY OF FEAR
ELOPE TO DEATH
ROGUE'S RANSOM
DEATH FROM BELOW
SLEEPY DEATH
NO NEED TO DIE
THE SNATCH
THE BIG CALL
THE MAN WHO STAYED ALIVE
THE SPEAKER
KILL OR BE KILLED
GIVE ME MURDER
WAIT FOR DEATH
COME HOME TO DEATH
BLACK FOR THE BARON
MISSING OR DEAD
A PROMISE OF DIAMONDS
THE BARON RETURNS
A BRANCH FOR THE BARON
BLAME FOR THE BARON
TRAP THE BARON
DEATH ON DEMAND
SHADOW THE BARON
A TASTE OF TREASURE
TERROR BY DAY
DEATH IN DIAMONDS
MURDER TOO LATE
DOUBLE FOR DEATH
A CASE FOR THE BARON
THE DARK CIRCLE
THE BARON AGAIN
A CLUTCH OF COPPERS
INVITATION TO ADVENTURE
DEATH ON THE MOVE
REWARD FOR THE BARON
ENGAGEMENT WITH DEATH
WARN THE BARON
SHADOW OF DEATH
VERSUS THE BARON
DARK MYSTERY
THE TOFF TAKES SHARES
THE TOFF ON BOARD
A KNIFE FOR THE TOFF
MEET THE BARON
CLOSE THE DOOR ON MURDER
THE TOFF IS BACK
A PUZZLE IN PEARLS
TWO MEN MISSING
MURDER WITH MUSHROOMS
A SCREAM OF MURDER
ACCUSE THE TOFF
THE TOFF AMONG THE MILL[illegible]
KILL THE TOFF
THE GALLOWS ARE WAITING
'WARE DANGER
ATTACK THE BARON
THE SECRET MURDER
HUNT THE TOFF
THE BARON AT LARGE
ALIAS THE BARON
MYSTERY MOTIVE
A RABBLE OF REBELS
LET'S KILL UNCLE LIONEL
CALL FOR THE BARON
MURDER MOST FOUL
DEATH IN FLAMES
DEATH IN HIGH PLACES
THE BARON COMES BACK
THE BARON AND THE BEGGAR
THE BARON RETURNS
THE TOFF AT BUTLIN'S
DON'T LET HIM KILL
A ROPE FOR THE BARON
NO NEED TO DIE
A LIFE FOR A DEATH
THE MAN WHO STAYED ALIVE
MURDER IN THE FAMILY
THREE FOR ADVENTURE

and published by Corgi Books

John Creasey

writing as Michael Halliday

Quarrel With Murder

CORGI BOOKS
A DIVISION OF TRANSWORLD PUBLISHERS LTD

QUARREL WITH MURDER

A CORGI BOOK 0 552 09837 X

Originally published in Great Britain
by Evans Bros.

PRINTING HISTORY
Evans Bros. edition published 1951
First paperback edition published 1957
Corgi revised edition published 1975

Corgi Books are published by Transworld Publishers Ltd.
Cavendish House, 57-59 Uxbridge Road,
Ealing, London, W.5.
Made and printed in Great Britain by
Hunt Barnard Printing Ltd., Aylesbury, Bucks.

Contents

Quarrel With Murder

CHAPTER I

Argument

'But,' said Anthony Grey, 'I didn't kill him.'

'Well,' answered Sarah Mellison, 'he's dead. No one else is about. Look!'

She tossed back her hair, burnished by the bright April sun to a fiery red. Grassland stretched for miles in all directions, rising to distant hills. The nearest tree was half a mile away.

To emphasise the obvious, the girl pointed and pirouetted round; if Tony Grey had needed proof that she was lovely, she proved it then.

'Look!' she repeated, emphatically. 'Not enough cover for a goat, let alone a lurking murderer!'

He repeated obstinately: 'But I didn't kill him.'

'Oh, don't stand there talking a lot of nonsense! If you didn't kill him, who did? Have you seen anyone else near?'

So she had the temper which is reputed to go with red hair. He had refused to suspect it before, being anxious not to imagine a blemish on so much perfection.

'Answer *that*,' said Sarah, witheringly.

He had some Celtic blood himself, and it rose sharply.

'I have seen someone else nearby,' he said coldly.

'Go on then, name them.'

'Look here – ' he began, and glanced down at the dead man, almost with impatience. Fate had played him the scurviest of tricks, producing this lifeless body on the first occasion when he had met Sarah on her own.

On her own? The glazed, blank eyes seemed to reproach him. There was no doubt that the man was dead.

'Why on earth did you do it?' Sarah asked with a certain show of reason.

'I've told you before, I didn't.'

'Oh, nonsense. If you can't name these people – '

'This person,' he corrected.

'Well, who was he?'

'She.'

'Who was she?'

Tony thrust one hand into his pocket, was tempted to look away from the gathering storm in her eyes, and managed to brazen it out. He kept his voice low; hoped it was steady.

'Miss Sarah Mellison,' he said.

There was a pause; then furiously the storm burst. She drew in her breath and raised a clenched hand, as if she would strike him. The colour drained away from her cheeks showing the freckles more clearly. She started to speak but no sound came, started again, her voice both shrill and unnatural.

'You beast,' she said. 'So you'd blame me! Of all the cowardly, miserable – '

'I didn't blame you!'

'Of course you blamed me. As if I – '

'I was simply pointing out the fact that we were both here. The possibility that I killed him is no greater than the possibility you did. You know that you didn't do it, I know that I didn't. So,' he shrugged, 'somebody else must have.'

'It didn't sound like that,' she said, more mildly. The storm had quietened, but was still nursed by hostility.

For the first time she really looked at the body. She shivered. A little frown drew a faint line between her eyes. She looked away again, and scanned the distant scene. Far off, someone appeared, but it was impossible to see whether it was a man or woman.

Tony took out his pipe, then his pouch, and slowly began to pack tobacco into the large, well-burned bowl. He congratulated himself on sounding normal.

'Supposing we stop arguing, and decide what we ought to do,' he said.

'Well, what ought we to do?' asked Sarah. She stared now towards the distant figure. The standing rays of the sun glinted on something bright, suggesting a bicycle. 'Someone's coming. I wish to heaven I'd never come out for a walk this afternoon!'

'It might have happened to anyone. If –'

'That doesn't mean that it had to be *me*,' breathed Sarah. Her voice was taut.

Tony had the imagination to see that she had come walking gaily across the commonland and come upon death; and it had shocked her. All she had since said had been due to that shock. He hadn't been normal, either, because there had been nothing normal in the circumstances. They had argued – quarrelled. The shock had lifted them out of their daily lives and they'd behaved like children. The truth hit him as with a sledge-hammer. Darkness descended upon his mind. Two living people beside a body of a young man, whose head had been smashed in. Little of the wound was visible from where Sarah stood, but when he had first come upon the body and seen it from the other side, the ugly, bloody mess had been all too clear.

'What are we going to do?' she whispered, and shivered again. Instinctively, they moved nearer to each other. Their hands touched; he didn't realise how it happened, but suddenly his arm was round Sarah's waist.

She was trembling.

'Take it easy,' Tony said.

'I can't. It's dreadful. You – you did say that he was still warm, didn't you?'

'Yes.'

He'd touched the outstretched hand. Strangely it wasn't until Sarah had arrived that he'd begun to feel conscious of shock; he'd seen death often enough. Nor had he begun to think of the oddness of the fact that he should have been found near the body, so soon after death.

'Don't you really know him?' Sarah whispered.

'I've never seen him before.'

'I wish I'd never seen him at all.'

The last words were so indistinct that he wasn't sure he heard them aright. She turned abruptly, her face buried itself against his shoulder, and she began to cry. In spite of the occasion, he felt both tender and a little ridiculous. He'd often met death, but seldom a crying woman. Her hair tickled his cheek and mouth, and he turned his head away. Then his free hand strayed up, and he found himself stroking her head.

Death – and life – so close together.

He now saw that the newcomer was a girl cyclist. There was a path across the common, and many people cycled across it, so there was nothing unusual in her coming. She was dark-haired, but too far away for him to tell whether he knew her or not. She had been in sight for a long time, and that emphasised the strangeness of the fact that no one except Sarah had been in sight when he had found the body.

'Take it easy,' he repeated. 'It's not as if we knew him, Sarah. Take it easy.'

Her crying became quieter.

'We'll have to tell the police,' he said. 'You'd better go, and I'll stay on guard. That's all we can do.'

She looked up, tears spoiling her beauty without taking away her charm.

'Will it mean – trouble?'

'Don't worry,' he said. 'We didn't kill him, there's no reason in the world why we should have killed him.'

'I wish I could sneak away and forget I'd seen him.'

'Well – '

'It'll be beastly.' She shivered again, and stole another look at the body. 'Police – inquests – talk. How they'll talk!' Now she blushed furiously. 'You don't know Wallingham well, you've only just come to live here. I've been here all my life. Well, nearly all.' Obviously she was talking partly for the sake of talking, and partly out of her fierce desire not to be mixed up in the inevitable consequences of this tragedy. 'They'll say I came to meet him by appointment.

They've always believed I'm a promiscuous little – '

She stopped abruptly, but not before she had startled him.

'Nonsense!'

'It isn't nonsense. Oh, some of them are all right, but most of them are jealous. I've got everything, and been everywhere, and they've gone on leading their own little dreary lives in the same monotonous way. They'll love this chance to gossip. They've gossiped enough already, the tales they tell – '

'I've heard no tales about you.'

'You've only been here for six weeks or so, they haven't started to confide in you yet,' she said. 'They'll take it for granted that I came to meet him, and even if the police don't, it will be *hell*!'

'Anyone who makes it hell isn't worth knowing.'

She took a small handkerchief from the pocket of her coat, and began to dab her eyes gently.

'Hell is hell,' she said, 'whoever makes it.' She was looking away from him, towards the cyclist. Tony realised that because the newcomer was riding into the evening sun, she couldn't see them. Her head was down, as if she were studying the ground in front of the wheel He doubted whether she knew that anyone else was in sight.

An idea flashed into his mind.

'Sarah – ' he began.

She looked up.

'You're probably right. There isn't any reason why the two of us should be mixed up in it. As you say, there's bound to be a lot of unpleasantness, but it will worry me much less than it will worry you. Why not slip off, now? No one need know that you came to this part of the common. I won't say anything.'

Suddenly her eyes shone.

'Do you mean that?'

'Of course I mean it.'

'But that girl – '

'She's still a couple of hundred yards away, and if you hurry, she won't recognise you. Walk straight into the sun all the way, and she probably won't know whether you're a man or a woman.'

'Well – '

'Hurry!' he urged.

She stretched out a hand and touched his. Her fingers were firm and her grip tight. She was very close to him for a moment, eyes still glistening, lips parted. In spite of her reddened eyes, she was beautiful.

'Thank you,' she whispered. 'I'll always be grateful.'

He stood and watched her go. She moved with the superb grace that had been the first thing he had noticed about her. When next they met they would have a secret shared by no one else. A grim secret, but – she had not seen the part of the young man's head where it was cracked like a shell.

The folly of what he had done did not dawn on him, then. He made himself look towards the cyclist, who was now forty or fifty yards away, with her head still down. She might even pass the spot without noticing him, because the path was thirty yards to his right. Then the front wheel wobbled, and righting the balance of the machine, she saw him. She clutched at the brakes sharply, and came to a standstill, slipping off the bicycle with practised ease. He did not remember having seen her before. She was small and dark, and rather striking.

'What – ' she began.

Then her gaze dropped, and she saw the dead man. Her hands left the bicycle, and it fell to one side; she ignored the crash. She stood like that, hands raised, body rigid, for what seemed an age. Then she darted past Tony and flung herself on her knees beside the body.

CHAPTER 2

Accusation

At first, she was silent; just stayed there on her knees, one of the dead man's hands in hers. She stared down. All Tony could see was her bowed head, her rigid shoulders and her legs, slim and shapely beneath a light grey skirt. It was an age before she moved.

He realised that she knew the man well. He expected an outburst of crying, far worse than Sarah's. But she did not cry. She released the lifeless hand and rested it gently on the grass, then turned round slowly. The sun shone fully on her, now. She had much of the beauty and vitality of Sarah Mellison, but an added grace, a maturity.

'Why did you kill him?' she asked flatly.

'I assure you – ' he began, and stopped. 'I assure you!' The phrase was absurdly formal, just didn't apply in circumstances like these. He was acting like a fool.

'Why did you kill him?' she asked again.

Was a second scene to repeat the first? If so, it was getting a little too monotonous for his liking. He said abruptly:

'I was walking across the common, and found him like this.'

'I don't believe you.'

With Sarah, he had lost his temper, with this girl he felt no temptation to lose it. Perhaps it was because there was more than shock; there was grief. It was obvious to him that she knew the man, and that meant a great deal to her.

'There's no reason in the world why I should have killed him,' he said reasoningly. 'I've never seen him before. I was going for the police, but saw you coming along. You'll be able to reach a telephone more quickly on your bicycle.'

'You killed him,' she said flatly.

'I m not going to argue with you. Will you hurry to the nearest telephone, and tell the police what's happened?'

'And leave you with him? No, I will not.'

'It's better that I should stay.'

She closed her eyes, as if a great weariness had come upon her, and she could not thrust it away. She hadn't Sarah's colouring, and had been pale all the time; now, she looked deathly white. She stood without speaking, for several minutes; he knew it was a long time. Then she opened her eyes.

'Have you a cigarette?'

'I'm sorry, I only smoke a pipe, and –'

'There are some in my bag,' she said, and went to her bicycle. She fumbled inside a small handbag, took out cigarettes and matches, lit a cigarette and put both packets back.

She drew nearer, slowly, and looked straight at him.

'I'm sorry I spoke like that,' she said, with an obvious effort at self-control. 'You see, he is my husband.' Her lips quivered, Tony felt his own throat tense and his eyes smart. It took her some time to steady her voice. 'I would rather that you called the police, and I stayed here.' The words came out in quick sentences, with a pause between each. 'I shall be all right. You needn't worry, I shall be all right.'

He had difficulty in speaking.

'You'll be so much quicker if you ride.'

'You ride,' she said. 'Please.' She turned away quickly, but not before he saw the quivering of her lips. Her shoulders shook, but she straightened them with sudden, swift, decision, and he heard no sound.

He went slowly to the bicycle. It was a woman's model, but there was no reason why he shouldn't ride it. Her handbag was still on the handlebars, and he took it off and put it on the grass. Then he looked at the girl again. She hadn't turned round, was staring into the distance – away from Sarah.

He could not see Sarah.

'I'm going,' he said gruffly.

She didn't answer.

He found it difficult at first. He hadn't cycled for years, and this light machine wobbled easily. But it was low enough for him to touch the ground with his feet and steady himself, if need be. Gathering speed over the rough path, he headed for the road to Wallingham.

The common stretched for miles, and the little town was nearly three miles away. The ground rose gently, and the slope hid the town itself, but when he had been cycling for five or six minutes, he saw the top of a church spire, clear and grey against the sky. Here, there were more trees, and more cover for a murderer to hide, but he did not think anyone had been here. He had walked in this direction, and would have seen anyone in sight. There was little undergrowth, and the trees, of silver birch and beech, were mostly young; they wouldn't hide a child. The slanting sun caught the silvered bark, making the scene beautiful – but never once driving the picture of that smashed-in head out of his mind.

He refused to let his thoughts run on; there was too much confusion in them. Sarah, the dead man and the dark-haired girl were all mixed up. It was not even possible to think clearly of Sarah. Now and again, he felt a twinge of doubt about the wisdom of letting her go. That wasn't the only cause of doubt.

If she were all he wanted to believe, would she have run away?

Forget it!

He could see the large houses on the western outskirts of the town, now, and the town itself, with red and grey roofed buildings spreading out on either side of the River Wall. The banks on this side were grassy, sloping down to the narrow river.

As he approached the road, a blue single-decker bus rattled along it, followed by two private cars. Drawing nearer, he saw several cyclists – among them, the erect figure of a policeman.

He pressed harder on the pedals.

The policeman, a biggish man, was heading for Wallingham. Tony shouted, but the cry was carried thinly away. He pressed harder, sweat dripping off his forehead. The policeman rode on, getting farther and farther away along the smooth surface of the road.

Tony stopped cycling, drew in a deep breath, and shouted: 'Oi!'

The policeman did not stop.

'Oi!' yelled Tony.

The man glanced round, without haste, and Tony waved. The policeman began to slow down. Tony shouted again. The policeman dismounted with slow deliberation. He was large, fleshy and young, his round face reddened by the recent fierce sunshine, his cheeks glistened with sweat. Yet his tunic was buttoned high at the neck and his helmet was in exactly the proper position.

'Did you call, sir?' he asked, from thirty yards away.

Was the man going to prove a fool?

'Yes. Hurry!'

Moving not one second faster for Tony's command, the policeman arrived at his elbow.

'What did you want, sir?'

How did one tell the story of finding a murdered man?

'Constable, I found – ' Tony broke off, as sweat trickled into his eye. He wiped it away, and felt angry with himself. He was a man of twenty-seven behaving like a schoolboy, and he'd had ample time to get over the shock. He must control himself. 'I found a dead man, on the common.'

Another trickle of sweat found its way into his eye.

Blankness on the policeman's face was followed by astonishment, tempered with caution.

'*Really*, sir?'

'I'm not fooling!' Tony said roughly.

'I'm sure you're not, sir. You found a – er – a dead man on the common. Had he been dead for long?'

'No. His head –'

Grey eyes, no longer ingenuous, looked at him warily. The policeman took a firmer grip on his bicycle.

'What about his head?'

'It's smashed in.'

'You mean, he'd been killed?'

'I think so. I was walking across the common, and –'

'I'll take your statement later,' said the constable. 'Just point out where the body is, and then telephone to the police station. Wallingham double-one-double-two. Ask for Superintendent Swanley. Can you remember that?'

'Yes, but wouldn't it be better if you –'

'I'll be glad if you'd do what I asked,' the constable said. 'Now, where's the body?'

Roger pointed.

'You'll strike the path soon, then you ride straight along it – west. You'll find the man and a girl.'

'A girl?'

'She came up afterwards. She said he was her husband. She wasn't there when I found the body, this is her bicycle. I think she came to meet him. Go easy with her.'

'You can leave that to me, sir. Double-one-double-two, and Superintendent Swanley. You won't forget will you? Have you sixpence?'

'Sixpence?'

'For the call.'

'Oh, yes. Yes, thanks.' Tony jingled coins in his pocket. 'Go easy with that girl.'

The constable did not answer, but mounted his bicycle and cycled off steadily, making good speed without appearing to hurry. Tony, cooler now, started off in search of a telephone kiosk. He found one within ten minutes. He called double-one-double-two and was answered at once.

'Yes, I'm Superintendent Swanley.'

'One of your men . . . ' Tony began, and stumbled through the end of his story.

Swanley, uttering no startled exclamation, seemed to take the news with infuriating calm. Would Mr Grey wait by the telephone booth? He would be along soon in a car, and they could go to the spot together.

Tony agreed perfunctorily. Now he had nothing to do but wait, and think.

He hadn't seen Sarah on the way. That was strange. He ought to have caught up with her. She must have gone in a different direction, possibly cut across to the back of one of these houses. The gardens, all of them walled, stretched out into the common; each had a private gate. He had no idea where Sarah lived; if in one of these, it would explain why he'd missed her.

Waiting was no fun, and he wasn't looking forward to being questioned by the police. If Sarah were with him and there was no need even for a white lie, it would have been easier. Why had she been so anxious to go? Had she set out to make him suggest it?

Suspecting her was fantastic, of course.

Was it?

He didn't notice the car until it was almost alongside. There were two men at the back, one with a suitcase on his knees. Why on earth bring a suitcase? At the wheel of the car, a recent model Austin 20, sat a well-dressed man with a long pointed nose. He glanced out of the window, and smiled; it was an amiable smile, which somehow gave the face strength.

'Mr Grey?'

'Yes.'

'I'm Swanley. Come and sit beside me, will you? I've another car coming behind, the driver will look after the bicycle.'

'Thanks.'

Tony climbed in. Before the door had closed, the car moved off; in that first moment he knew that Swanley was an exceptional driver.

'Now, tell me all about it,' Swanley said. 'What you found, who else was on the common – anything you noticed. Take your time.' He smiled again, and waited.

CHAPTER 3

Difficulties

Tony looked straight ahead as he told the story. He had to guard his tongue carefully, to make sure that he dropped no hint that anyone else had been with him. Swanley made no comment, but turned off the road where Tony told him, and drove across the common. The car lurched from side to side, but the springing was good, there was no need to stop the recital. When he'd finished, they were a hundred yards or so away from the constable, the dark-haired girl and the body.

They drew up.

The girl looked at them without much interest. Colour and emotion seemed to have been drained from her face. Her eyes were sad, their expression hurtful.

The constable saluted.

'I've made some preliminary enquiries, sir. The lady is Mrs Denton, the deceased's name was Raymond Denton.'

'That's good,' said Swanley, and went across to the girl. She couldn't be much more than twenty-two or three. 'I'm very sorry about this,' he said, and sounded as if he meant it. 'So he's your husband.'

'Yes.'

'We'll cause you as little distress as we can,' promised Swanley. 'Would you like to go into town, and wait for me there?'

She hesitated, took another glance at the body, and then said: 'Yes – yes, I would.'

'You're wise,' Swanley said. 'Parker – ' he spoke to one of the men from the back of the car, who was now opening the suitcase. 'You drive back, will you, see that Mrs Denton is comfortable, and give the go ahead on Operation 2. We're going to search the common,' he added to the girl. 'I won't leave you at the station a moment longer than I must. Is there anyone else who ought to be informed at once?'

'Not here,' she said. 'Ray had no close relatives. Mine – mine can wait.' She shivered. 'But if my landlady can be told that I won't be back for a few hours, it will stop her from worrying.'

'Give Sergeant Parker the address, and he'll see to it,' said Swanley.

She went off, with Parker. He was a large man with broad shoulders, and the woman looked tiny beside him. He opened the door for her, next to the driver's seat, obviously about to excel Swanley in courtesy. There was no harshness about any of this; Tony wondered vaguely why he had expected to find some.

The car moved off unsteadily.

'Now, Bennett.' Swanley turned to the constable. 'What's your report?'

Bennett was bursting to talk, Tony anxious to listen while finding his attention distracted by the activities of the man who had remained with them. He was setting out a number of articles on the grass; a tape measure, a hammer, some wooden pegs, a large camera.

Bennett was saying: 'I found everything as Mr Grey informed me, sir, and when I arrived, the young lady was standing by the body, looking over there.' He pointed in the direction from which the girl had come. 'I spoke to her, and she didn't seem to hear me. Seemed to be in a kind of trance, sir. So I touched her shoulder, and she jumped – quite gave me a turn, she was so frightened.'

'Frightened,' Swanley said musingly.

'Yes, sir – pale as death, she was. I reassured her, and she made no difficulties of any kind. She volunteered her name, and said that she had been married for three weeks. Just *three weeks*.' P.C. Bennett revealed the romantic in him with his emphasis. 'They haven't a home of their own, as yet; he was looking for one. She lives in Hoodle, and works at Corby & Corby's store. She had time off this afternoon to go and look at some rooms, but they were too expensive. She knew her husband would be in town, and cycled to see him, as she had another address to go to.'

Swanley was watching the plainclothes man, who was now preparing the camera for photographs, but was obviously paying close attention to Bennett's story. 'Did she expect to meet him on the common?'

'No, in town, sir.' Bennett pointed with a large, clean hand. 'But apparently they often met here in the evenings, by that tree with the broken branch. He'd been out to look at a flat, over at Salisbury – she doesn't know whether he had any luck or not.'

'What did he do for a living?'

'Travelling salesman, sir. Rather a funny thing, she didn't seem to know much about it. They met about three months ago, love at first sight, she said.'

Swanley looked at him intently.

'Did she use those words?'

'Well, sir – ' Bennett broke off, colouring.

'Don't put words into her mouth. We've to get at facts, Bennett. I want you to make a full report quickly, and have it ready for me when I get back. You'd better get off.'

'Yes, sir.' A crestfallen Bennett went across to his bicycle.

Another car was coming up, with five men in it. The sun was sinking, and while it was still daylight, the brightness had gone and long shadows stretched across the grassland.

The gloom was suddenly brightened by a flash, as the photographer took his first picture. The other men drew up, and Swanley gave them instructions crisply. One man drove the pegs into the ground round the body, and then began to measure the distance from each peg to an arm, a leg, a shoulder and the head. Another drew a rough diagram, and noted the distances as the other called them out. A third was examining the girl's bicycle, which was on the back of the second police car. Two others were looking at the ground, as if searching for something which had been dropped.

Swanley turned to Tony.

'What were you doing out here, Mr Grey?'

'I often walk across the common.'

'So early in the afternoon? You must have started soon after three o'clock.'

'I did. I prefer walking in the afternoon.'

'Don't you work?' Swanley smiled.

'I write,' said Tony abruptly. This was a tender spot, and he saw no reason to go into details. 'I do most of my work in the mornings and evenings.'

'Oh, I see. What brought you in this direction?'

The simple truth was that he had heard that Sarah Mellison often walked across the common in the afternoon, and had hoped to come across her. He couldn't say that.

'I might have gone anywhere,' he said at last. 'I'd been out as far as Hoodle – I didn't go into the village, just as far as the church – and came back this way. That made a round trip, I didn't need to go over the same ground twice.'

'I see.' Swanley seemed to be giving most of his attention to the men. 'Bad luck, to walk into this. Do you know Mrs Denton?'

'I've never seen her before.'

'Denton?'

'No.'

'He looks a nice young chap,' said Swanley. 'About your build, too.'

Denton still lay in exactly the same position. His hair was fair, wavy and, on this side, untouched by blood. He had a broad nose and a good, square chin. He looked powerful, and was probably in the early thirties. An open air, athletic type, from the look of him – and 'nice young chap' seemed to describe him aptly.

Swanley glanced round, and for the first time, Tony noticed other men approaching, a dozen of them on bicycles, swaying over the common and along the path.

'We're going to search,' Swanley said. 'We'll be able to do

a bit by daylight, and then we'll probably have to lay off until morning. You say you saw no one else at all?'

'That's so.'

'Quite sure?'

'Of course I'm sure!'

He could picture Sarah's red head and realised his own folly more clearly. To save her from embarrassment he had risked being caught out in a lie; the police were not fools. It was his own fault, if he'd insisted, she would have stayed.

'You think you arrived soon after he was killed,' Swanley said.

'It looked like that.'

'How long do you think he'd been dead?'

'It's impossible to say.' Perhaps the police *were* fools, after all. 'When I first saw him, I thought he was asleep. It wasn't until I glanced round from the other side, and saw the wound, that I realised he was dead.'

'I suppose he *was* dead.'

Tony flared up.

'What do you mean?'

'Easy,' said Swanley. 'I'm not suggesting that you found him in glowing health! But he seemed to be asleep – is it possible that he died after you found him?'

'I don't think so. He could have been dead for half-an-hour or so, I suppose – and given someone plenty of time to get away.'

'You seemed so sure that he hadn't been dead long.'

'That's how it seemed to me,' Tony said. 'I touched his hands, and they were warm – as warm as mine.'

'They're still warm,' said Swanley. 'But as you didn't see anyone else about, why was it you assumed that he'd been killed so recently? If you'd seen someone near you might have assumed that was the killer, but –'

Tony said: 'I don't know why it sprang to my mind.'

He did know; it was because, subconsciously, he had feared that Sarah had killed the man. But now that he began to think rationally, there was no reason why. She'd had no weapon, and some heavy instrument must have been used to crack the man's head in. He'd seen no weapon lying near; that was undoubtedly what the policemen were looking for.

'The mind does queer things,' Swanley said, absently. 'How long have you lived in Wallingham?'

'Six weeks.'

'And you know the common well?'

'Fairly well,' said Tony. 'I know there's nowhere to hide, anyhow.' He looked round at the darkening scene, but could still see for hundreds of yards in each direction. Another car was lurching towards them.

'Hmm,' said Swanley. 'Didn't you forget the trenches?'

'Trenches?'

'Yes. Never mind.' Swanley turned away as the other car stopped.

A man climbed out, so tall and lean that he seemed to uncoil himself as he stood up. At full height, he towered over Swanley, who wasn't far short of six feet. But for his thinness, he would have been good looking; as it was, he was striking enough, with a hooked nose, bony chin and deeply indented cheeks.

He took a black case out of the car, waving his free hand in casual greeting.

'Hallo,' he said, and his voice was surprisingly deep; Tony had expected reedy tones. 'Why choose today?'

'Sorry,' Swanley said, 'the murderer didn't consult me. This is Mr Grey, who found the body. Mr Grey, Dr Asterley. All yours, Rick.'

'Have you touched him at all?'

'No – I haven't even looked in his pockets.'

'I always said you were a remarkable man, for a policeman,' said Dr Asterley. 'Possessed of great restraint.' He smiled vaguely; but perhaps not so vaguely, Tony could have sworn that his right eyelid flickered. 'Found the weapon?'

'No.'

'I suppose you want me to tell you exactly what was used,' said Asterley, ironically.

He went down on one knee beside the body. Then he seemed to forget everyone else, and his long, bony fingers began to prod and probe. Tony turned away abruptly, conscious of Swanley's protracted stare. Swanley wasn't satisfied that he had told the truth.

The men who had arrived on bicycles were now widely dispersed. One shouted unexpectedly, and next moment his head appeared about the level of the ground. He was about two hundred yards away, but clearly visible, scrambling out of a hole in the ground; a *trench*? The word had a sickening impact on Tony. He realised the significance of it. He hadn't known that there were trenches across the common, and yet had pretended that he knew it well. Had that been true, he could hardly have failed to have known about the trenches. The lie had only been necessary because of Sarah Mellison.

The man was waving something, a small yellowish bat, rather like an Indian club. As he drew nearer, Tony saw that he was holding it with the utmost care, a handkerchief wrapped round the handle.

He was breathing hard.

'Not much doubt about *that*,' he said triumphantly, and thrust the thing forward. There was blood at the end, and on one side. 'No doubt at all, is there, sir?'

'I shouldn't think so,' said Swanley, thoughtfully. 'A baseball bat – that ought to be a help. Do you play baseball, Mr Grey?'

CHAPTER 4

The Weapon

It wasn't the question or the way it was asked which affected Tony, but its obvious significance. Swanley couldn't have said more clearly : 'I think you may know more about this than you've admitted.'

'No,' Tony said shortly.

'I shouldn't think there are many in Wallingham,' said Swanley. He took the bat from the other man, and studied it carefully. The headlights of a car shone on the sinister, dull brown stains. 'Wrap it up and put it in my car. Anything else?'

'Not yet, sir,' said the policeman. 'The ground is powerful hard.'

'Yes. Pity. Carry on for half-an-hour, then we'll have another go at it tomorrow. Tell the others they can go straight home, unless they've anything to report.'

'Thank you, sir.' The man went off.

It was getting colder, now that the sun was gone and there was only the afterglow in the sky. The stars were showing faintly in the east, and a soft wind was blowing.

Dr Asterley, gaunt in the headlights of a car, straightened up and came towards them.

'He's dead,' he said, in a brief, official voice.

'The blow on the head?'

'As far as I can see, yes, but I'll have a look at him on the bench. *Rigor* hasn't started yet, but it soon will in this falling temperature. I'd get him away.'

'The ambulance should soon be here,' said Swanley, and looked towards the road. There, car headlights were moving swiftly, lighting up the night. One of the beams turned towards them, moving up and down, ghostly against trees and hillocks. 'This will be it. Care to give Mr Grey a lift back, Rick?'

'Always glad to help,' said Asterley. 'But I'm not staying in your mausoleum tonight. I have life as well as death to attend, and I haven't had my tea. I refuse to miss it. Deliver the corpse to the morgue and I'll look in when I can.'

'Before dinner,' Swanley said firmly.

'Ghoul,' said Asterley. 'Have you had tea, Mr Grey?'

'No, I –'

'Then we shall drink together,' said Asterley. 'Don't tell the policeman, but I know a little place where you can get real cream, and tea as it should be made.' He put a hand on Tony's arm, guiding him to his car.

It was good to sit back and relax.

Asterley put his bag in the back, and they drove off, stopping at a small cottage with two lighted windows.

'Here we are.'

Asterley opened the door, and they climbed out. It was by now quite dark, but a lovely clear night. No other traffic was in sight, and the light at the cottage windows was softened by curtains. The door opened before they reached it, and a girl stood there, the background light making a nimbus of her hair.

'Hallo, Meg. Am I too late?'

'Why, no, Doctor, come in.'

'I've a friend with me.'

'We're always glad to see a friend of yours,' said the girl, and looked at Tony with frank approval. 'Come you in, now.'

The room was small, and had a low ceiling. There were four small tables, now unoccupied. Meg left them, and Tony studied the homely bric-a-brac on corner brackets. Asterley went across to the log fire, his head bent because upright he would have touched the ceiling, and rubbed his hands.

'Come and thaw out, Grey.' He offered a battered cigarette case.

The light from a single lamp on one of the tables added to the fire's glow. The room was warm and cosy, and drove unpleasant visions away. Tony wondered why Swanley had allowed him to come. Asterley wasn't a policeman, but was obviously a close friend of the Superintendent; and shrewd. That he would try to draw out the truth might be part of Swanley's plan of campaign.

Asterley smiled. He had good teeth, and his smile took away from the gauntness of his face.

'Dead man a friend of yours?'

'No – a stranger.'

'Good!' Perhaps it hadn't been a trick question. 'Nothing more gruelling than to go through a job like this when it's someone you know. I've seen you about, but you're new in Wallingham, aren't you?'

'Yes. An aunt of mine died a few months ago, and left me a house here. I moved in, to find out how I liked country life.' They were simple facts, anyhow.

Asterley's eyes widened.

'You're not Matilda Henderson's nephew, Tony?'

'I am, indeed.'

'Well, well!' said Asterley. 'We're really old friends. I looked after her. She often talked about you, said that you were the idiot of the family, the perpetual rebel and the only one worth helping. Shrewd, too.' Asterley chuckled. 'I remember her saying that you had the wanderlust because you'd no anchorage, and she said she would provide the anchorage and then see how you behaved.'

'Oh,' said Tony, uncertainly. 'I seldom saw her, I didn't know she was interested. She'd been ill for some time, hadn't she?'

'Years. How she kept going I don't know. The spirit is stronger than the flesh. She was a loss to Wallingham, few people did more good. She left a lot of money to the Church and charities, as, of course, you must know. Annoyed about that?'

Tony laughed at the unexpectedness of the question.

'Good Lord, no! The house was more than I dreamed of

getting. Some of my relatives were a bit sore, I believe, but – ' he broke off, for the door opened and the girl brought in tea.

Asterley had not boasted without cause. There was cream, home-made jam, hot scones, plenty of butter. She placed the tray on a table by the fire, and Tony was surprised to find how hungry he was, then realised that it was after six o'clock.

Asterley kept up a running commentary, amusing, irrelevant. He didn't mention the inheritance again. There was nothing really surprising in the fact that it was he who had treated Aunt Matilda; there couldn't be many doctors in Wallingham, with its population of six thousand.

'More tea?' Asterley poured out. 'We'll have to be getting back. Feeling more yourself?'

'Much, thanks.'

'But not too much,' Asterley said knowingly. 'Shock works in the strangest ways.' He smiled. 'Don't elaborate anything with my friend Swanley until you feel completely on top of yourself. Police get queer ideas. If you didn't kill this chap, there's no reason why you should get yourself suspected. Any friends in Wallingham?'

'No.'

'Anywhere?'

'Not really close friends,' said Tony. 'That's one of the consequences of wanderlust. I've been out of England quite a bit. I know several languages, and got jobs abroad, but couldn't settle.'

'Miss Henderson said something about the writing bug.'

Tony laughed.

'Any luck?'

'No. Mine is an elusive talent, I sometimes wonder if it's there at all. I'm hoping that I can settle down here for a bit, and find out. I planned to give myself a year's trial, and if I've done nothing then, I'll probably sell the house and start moving again.'

'Sound idea,' said Asterley. 'Well! Anything I can do at any time, I will. Not for the sake of your brown eyes, but for Miss Henderson's!' He laughed as he uncoiled himself from the armchair, then ducked to avoid the ceiling. 'That's the one disadvantage here, they forget that some men really grow up! I'll drop you at the Station, I ought to look in and see Swanley again, if he's back.'

'Thanks,' said Tony.

'Pleasure.' Asterley grinned.

Wallingham Police Station was in a side street, an ugly Victorian building, with a blue lamp outside bearing the one word: *Police*. Four stone steps led to a bleak entrance hall. No one was in sight, but a door stood open on the right, showing a barely furnished room with a hatless police sergeant sitting at a desk.

'Visitor for you,' Asterley called out. 'He'll look after you, Grey.' He clapped Tony on the shoulder, and then turned towards a stone staircase which faced the front door.

The sergeant looked up from his writing, and stretched his cramped fingers. He was stout and elderly, and his eyes looked tired.

'Evening, sir. Mr Grey, isn't it?'

'Yes.' He had probably been warned that Tony would come with the police surgeon. 'Is Mr Swanley in?'

'He won't keep you long, sir, come in and take a chair. Cold after the sun goes in, isn't it? Care for a cup of tea?'

'No, thanks.'

'He won't keep you waiting long,' repeated the sergeant, and turned to the desk and laborious writing.

Dr Asterley knocked on the door of the Superintendent's office, and went inside. The room was long and narrow. Two fluorescent lighting strips shone on Swanley's thin hair and gave his face an unnatural pallor as he sat in a swivel chair behind a large, flat-topped desk. He glanced up with a smile.

'Sit down, Rick.' He waved to a chair.

Asterley sat. 'Any good tidings?'

'Not yet. How did you get on with young Grey?'

'Nice lad, if lad's the word,' said Asterley. 'Suffering from shock.'

'So I thought. No reason why a healthy young man should suffer to such a degree as that, is there? Struck me he wasn't telling the whole truth. It may mean something or nothing, but –'

'He certainly didn't give anything away to me. You might like to know that he's a nephew of –'

'Miss Matilda Henderson,' said Swanley blandly. 'I knew where he lived, and it was easy to dig that up. He doesn't seem to have made many friends in the town yet.'

'A man needs six years to make friends in Wallingham!'

'Oh, it's not as bad as that,' said Swanley. 'Anyhow, we'll find out whether he knew the Dentons or not, that's only a matter of time. Think Mrs Denton has the strength to use that baseball bat?' The question came out sharply.

'Haven't studied her muscular development,' said Asterley. 'The one thing you can be sure of is that it was someone the dead man knew. There was no sign of a struggle, just a smashing blow on the side of his head. I'd say the killer hit him again four or five times. Odd, that – nothing frenzied about the attack, just a series of calculated blows by someone who knew how to use the weapon. But you've realised all that, of course. I suppose you've also realised that the body was moved, after the attack, and turned over. Otherwise the wounds would have been on the top side.'

Swanley nodded. Asterley grinned.

'Up to you to guess why he was moved, but I'd say that it was because the killer wanted to go through his pockets. Find anything on the body?'

'Nothing that helps,' said Swanley, 'and no evidence of robbery, there are seven or eight pound notes in his wallet. In fact the only curious thing is this,' he went on, and handed Asterley an envelope. 'Six photographs, of six young and attractive women. You might glance through them and tell me if you've ever seen any of them before.'

3

CHAPTER 5

Six Pretty Pictures

The interlude with Asterley, followed by a wait of twenty minutes in the charge room, did Tony good. His pipe was going smoothly, and there was something reassuring about the steady movements of the sergeant's hand and the faint scratching sound of pen on paper. It was possible to ponder over the events of the evening dispassionately, to judge the strength and weakness of what he had told Swanley. It had only one real weakness, and there was no reason why that should be damaging.

He heard a man coming down the stairs. Asterley passed with long strides, waving as he went. A few seconds afterwards, the Talbot moved off. There was little noise outside; the police station was in a backwater, a hundred yards from the main road.

The telephone bell rang, and the sergeant eased his fingers again before taking off the receiver.

'Yes, sir' he said deferentially. 'Yes, sir, at once, sir.' He put the receiver down, and called: 'Bob!'

A young policeman put his head round the inner doorway.

'Take this gentleman up to the Superintendent, at once.'

'Right!'

Tony followed his brisk lead into the gloomy hall and up the stone steps. He felt no qualms; why should he? Pipe still drawing well, he stepped inside Swanley's office, meeting the Superintendent's eye with cool self-possession.

'Ah, Mr Grey. Sorry I had to keep you.'

'That's all right.'

'Enjoy your tea?'

'Dr Asterley's a man worth knowing.'

'He is indeed,' said Swanley, quite seriously. 'Come and sit down. All right, constable.'

'Mind if I smoke?' asked Tony.

'I'm going to, myself.' Swanley took a cigarette but didn't light it. 'I don't think I need keep you much longer. I've had a statement drawn up based on what you've already told me. I'll get you to read it through in a few minutes, and sign if you approve.'

Tony grinned. 'And supposing I don't?'

'Then we'll alter it,' said Swanley, settling back comfortably in his chair. He looked very much at home, capable, reassuring. 'Ever had much to do with newspapermen?'

'Not much.'

'You'll probably be worried by them tonight and tomorrow. If they get too persistent, let me know and I'll try to fend them off. There's no reason why you shouldn't answer their questions, I'm issuing a statement to the Press a little later. Not that I'm very worried about you, but Mrs Denton will probably find it a strain.'

'I suppose so,' Tony said, a little more warily. Swanley surely did not mean to go on being so amiable.

'I'm sorry for her,' Swanley said, with great deliberation. 'She appears to be quite friendless. They'd only been married a few weeks.' He lit his cigarette, then picked up an envelope and handed it across the desk. 'Have a look at those, will you?'

Here was the catch.

Tony felt the envelope; there were cards inside, about the size of postcards. He drew them out, and all were face downwards. There was no reason why he should feel nervous; he was quite steady as he turned them over. The face of a girl, young, attractive, but unfamiliar, looked up at him. He put that photograph aside, and saw the face of another girl, with fluffy hair and a simpering smile. Conscious of Swanley's intent gaze, he looked up.

'What am I supposed to be doing?'

'Seen either of them before?'

'No.'

Tony turned to the third photograph, did not recognise the girl, was glancing at the fourth when he thought of Sarah. He felt himself tense, and stared more intently at the picture. This fourth girl seemed younger than any of the others, and had a heart-shaped face, cupid's bow lips; she would have looked perfect on a chocolate box.

The fifth and sixth were also of attractive girls.

'No,' he said, 'I don't think I've seen any of them before. There's one – ' he turned back to Number 4, for Swanley would have noticed his reaction. 'I thought I recognised her – a French girl I used to know. But it's not her, I'm sure of that.' He handed the photographs back and smiled.

'You've travelled a lot, haven't you?'

'A fair amount.'

'Getting material for your books?'

Tony grinned.

'There aren't any books, there's just a dream of one. I've written a few articles and had a short story published once, but don't get the idea that I'm a fully fledged writer. My aunt left me the house in Middle Street, and I'm seeing if I can do better in a country town.'

'The Muse takes a lot of prompting,' Swanley said mildly. 'No other attractions in Wallingham?'

'I'd hardly heard of the place – knew vaguely that my aunt lived here, that's all.'

'Made any friends since you arrived?'

'I couldn't say friends. The first thing I did was to join the Amateur Dramatic Society, they were appealing for new members for some summer performances. So I've met a few people, but Wallingham's rather a closed shop, isn't it?'

'You'll soon get it opened.' Swanley sat back and pressed the tips of his fingers together. 'But I'm forgetting my job!' He handed Tony some typewritten sheets of paper.

They had put his statement into simple language, and nothing had been added. He took out his pen and signed.

'Thanks.' Swanley put the statement aside. 'The mind is a

funny thing, Mr Grey, and you had a sharp shock. You may find when you've rested a bit that things you hadn't noticed will come back to you. If they do, let me know at once, please.'

'Such as?' asked Tony.

'I'm not going to make suggestions, I don't want to influence you. Just think over everything you saw and remember. Obviously, I'm most interested in getting a description of anyone who was on Hoodle Common about the time that you were. Without remembering now, you may have noticed two or three people leaving the common as you reached it. Or you may have seen someone in the distance whom you didn't recognise – anything like that. In fact, anything at all. I – '

He broke off, abruptly.

'Yes?' Tony said.

Swanley glanced towards a table in a corner. On it were several things Tony hadn't noticed before. A wallet, some loose change, a watch, a pen-knife, two ivory dice and, standing upside down and resting against the wall, the baseball bat. It was partly covered by the handkerchief he had to look at it hard to be sure what it was.

'Hand me that bat, will you?' Tony was nearer than Swanley. 'It's all right, it's been tested for prints, but no luck.' Tony got up and fetched it. There was a smear of grey powder on the handle and on the club. The head hadn't been cleaned . . . Tony brought it across, feeling slightly sick, and Swanley took it in both hands. 'You say you don't play baseball.'

'No.'

'Have you seen a bat like this before?'

'Several times – I've met a lot of Americans. Most of them are mustard keen on the game.'

'Seen one lately?'

'I can't say I – ' Tony began, and then broke off abruptly. 'Why, yes! At the Theatre Club. They've an American play in rehearsal, two or three baseball bats are used as props. I've noticed – '

Swanley jumped up, cutting across his words.

'I just remembered that, too.' He pressed a bell-push in his desk, and stretched across for his hat. 'Can you spare half-an-hour?'

'If it will help.'

'It might.' Swanley looked at the door, which was opened by a tall, middle-aged man whose right arm hung stiffly by his side. 'Clarke, telephone Mrs McNaughton and ask her to meet me at the Theatre Club in the next half-hour – as early as she can make it.'

'Yes, sir.'

'We'll get off,' Swanley said. 'It's well after seven, there's usually someone at the club at this time. My daughter's a member, that's how I come to know so much about it.' He put a hand on Tony's arm, to usher him into the passage and down the stairs. His grip was firm; it was almost as if he were making sure that Tony couldn't get away.

They hurried down the stairs, then turned left through a long passage, and out to the yard at the back of the police station. A black Maria van was drawn up at one end, and there were several private cars, two with a 'Police' sign on the roof. Swanley's Austin was nearest the gate.

They started off.

'If no one is there, you can show me round,' Swanley said. That was a belated and lame excuse for taking Tony with him. 'You haven't a part in this play, I suppose?'

'I don't think I'm likely to get a part in any play for a long time.'

'Closed shop again, eh?' Swanley chuckled.

They turned right and drove through dark streets where the houses were tall and narrow and opened straight on to the side walk. Then they swung into a quiet square, flanked by warehouses. Here, a lighted doorway bore the sign: Wallingham Theatre Club. On each side of the club was a narrow alley leading to the river.

They stepped out, on to cobbled stones.

'Can't expect Mrs McNaughton to be here yet,' Swanley said. 'Do you know her?'

'I couldn't fail to! She *is* the club!'

Swanley chuckled again.

The steady ping-pong sound of table tennis came clearly as they went in; it was played in a room on the right. This was a large, barely-furnished games room; the Theatre Club was also a Social Club which was becoming increasingly popular. They glanced into the room. A plump girl wearing a white jumper stretched tightly across her ample figure, was playing a youngster of fifteen or so. Three other girls and a boy were watching.

'Are they actually rehearsing this American play now?' Swanley said.

'Dress rehearsals start this week.'

'I'm not sure where the stage is,' said Swanley. 'Upstairs or down?'

'Up.' The stairs were of creaky wood, the walls bare. The whole of the top floor was the 'theatre' with a good stage at one end, comfortable chairs stretched across in front of it. There was seating for three hundred people. The stage lighting was good, the McNaughton family and others with money had spared nothing to make it a real attraction. One disadvantage was that the stage could only be reached through the auditorium – there were doors on either side. On the right were the men's dressing-rooms, on the left, the women's. Tony led the way to the men's, then on to the stage itself.

It was set for an outdoor scene, the scenery painted to resemble an old-fashioned wooden Colonial house, with tall pillars. There were few props. Two metal tables, eight chairs, a garden seat and a pair of wooden steps leading off stage seemed to be the lot. On one chair were two tennis racquets, and on the floor by another, three baseball bats.

'How many are used?' Swanley asked abruptly.

'I don't know.'

'Sure?'

'Of course I'm sure.'

Swanley's gaze raked the stage, and came to rest on the door in the wings which led from the other dressing-room.

'I'll be glad when Mrs McNaughton comes, she'll know if one is missing.'

'I suppose so,' Tony said.

A head appeared; a red head.

Sarah Mellison glanced startlingly at them, then withdrew abruptly.

CHAPTER 6

Mrs McNaughton

'I'm not sure how many baseball bats are in a set,' Swanley said, 'or whether set is the right word. I believe the big name players have dozens of the things. Do you know anything about the play?'

'No, I haven't seen a script.'

'Pity.' Swanley showed no further interest in the dressing-room, and had been too intent on watching the door to notice Tony's expression when he had recognised Sarah. 'How many people in the cast?'

'There's a script over there,' Tony said.

It was lying on a chair, a dog-eared copy in a blue cover. The play was called 'The Last Game', and a cast-list was in front of the cyclostyled script. He scanned it.

'Nine,' he said, 'and three walking-on parts.' He added: 'And I wonder how many others are familiar with the script.'

'If you mean, how many would know that baseball bats are used, probably twenty or more people. You know, there's no justification for assuming that it was one of these bats.'

'Oh, no.' Swanley was almost airy. 'Have to make sure. Let me have a look at the cast, will you?' He took the script and began to read in a voice Tony could just hear. 'Patrick McNaughton, Ken Sinclair, Sarah Mellison – that was Miss Mellison we saw just now, wasn't it?'

'Yes.'

'She's early, rehearsals don't start until half-past seven, do they? Let me see – John Liddel, May Curtis, Jack – '

He broke off.

'Hal-*lo*!' a woman called in a strident voice. 'Hal-*lo*!' A door banged, someone walked heavily along the gangway leading to the men's dressing-rooms. 'Anyone about?' The strident voice echoed in the empty hall. 'Hal*lo*, there!' The woman stumped heavily up the stone steps leading to the stage. 'Drat the man! Says it's urgent, and then keeps me waiting. Policemen! How he ever came to have a nice girl like Millicent for a daughter I don't know. What does he want, anyhow?' The door leading from the auditorium to the wings burst open and banged back. 'Hal – oh, *there* you are.'

Mrs McNaughton had arrived.

Wherever Mrs McNaughton appeared, everyone within earshot knew it; and all except those with very short sight, saw it. Almost square of figure, tightly corsetted, she appeared to like bright, even startling, colours. Diamonds glinted and sparkled, flashing in all directions.

'Why didn't you answer?' she demanded.

'You didn't give us much time.' Swanley smiled. 'Very nice of you to come so quickly.'

'Do you mean to tell me there *wasn't* any need to hurry?' The time-worn face was heavily rouged and deeply lined, a tragedy of the consequences of unskilful face-lifting.

'Oh, there was,' Swanley said hastily. 'We –'

Mrs McNaughton dropped heavily on to a chair.

'Those stairs. I'll murder that landlord one day. Or should it be the Town Clerk or the Engineer? *One* of them won't let us alter the place. It's fantastic. Superintendent, you carry some authority in this town, can't *you* do anything about it? We've the money, it wouldn't take much material, and the theatre would be twice as popular if the auditorium were downstairs.'

'It's hardly my province –'

'Oh, you *officials*.' Mrs McNaughton sniffed, and opened an expensive crocodile handbag, and took out a crumpled packet of cigarettes. 'I suppose I'll have to organise a petition before I get it. Red tape!' She stuck a cigarette into a holder and rummaged in the bag for matches.

Swanley flicked a lighter and held it out.

'You're nearly always full, so it can't make much difference.'

'I still have to walk up those damned stairs, don't I?' Mrs McNaughton lit her cigarette. 'Well, suppose you tell me why you've dragged me out in the middle of dinner. It's bad enough eating early because of these rehearsals, if they'd only do what they're told they wouldn't need so many or have to be here so early.' She added sharply: *'Is it the murder?'*

She had well-shaped eyes, light grey, bold, piercing; her one good feature.

'Yes,' said Swanley.

'Well, none of *my* pupils did it.'

'I haven't suggested – '

'Of course you've suggested it,' Mrs McNaughton snapped impatiently. '*Everyone* knows you've come here, and if they don't, they soon will. Why didn't you come to see me at my house?'

'I needed to see you here, because – '

'It's a waste of time, and nothing you say will convince me it's not. A waste of *my* time, a waste of *your* time and that means the tax-payers' money, and – ' Mrs McNaughton broke off, fixing Tony with her penetrating stare. 'What are you doing here? I didn't know you were in the cast.'

'The Superintendent asked me – '

'How many baseball clubs should be among the props?' asked Swanley gently. He went across and picked one up.

Mrs McNaughton looked at the club in his hand, torn between a desire to appear unhelpful and a professional knowledge of her own terrain.

'Four.'

'Then I want to find the fourth,' said Swanley, vigorously. 'May I use the telephone?' There was one in the wings and he didn't wait for permission but strode across the stage.

Mrs McNaughton glowered at Tony.

'Why on earth did you bring him here?'

'He brought me.'

'In trouble?' asked Mrs McNaughton, in an undertone so low that Tony hardly heard it.

'No, I happened – '

'Found the body, didn't you?'

'Yes.'

'Don't let that man fool you,' continued Mrs McNaughton. 'He's a snake in the grass, I've never liked him. While organising endless trouble for innocent motorists who happened to leave their cars in the parking place for five minutes over the hour, he lets a man get murdered. Now he tries to blame someone for it.'

She stopped, suddenly aware that Swanley could be heard on the telephone. He was asking for three men to be sent round at once.

'He'll ruin the rehearsal,' cried Mrs McNaughton, her voice rising to its natural pitch.

'We'll be just as quick as we can,' Swanley said soothingly. 'You can be a great help, Mrs McNaughton. Who – '

'*I* know nothing about it.' Mrs McNaughton stood up and backed towards the footlights, so abruptly that she seemed in danger of falling over them. 'What do you *want?*'

'That fourth baseball bat.'

'Oh is that all?' babbled Mrs McNaughton. 'Then let me tell you that that play was a bad choice. I let the Committee have its own way, but I warned them. If you put that American thing on, I told them, you'll have trouble. It'll be a flop. Oh, it's a good play, but imagine the mess they'll make of the accent. The only player who can talk American is Sarah, but she can't carry the whole cast.'

'Sarah who?' asked Swanley, very quietly.

'Mellison. She's the only Sarah in the club – sometimes I think she's the only actress, too. It's a pity she's so conceited.'

'It's a pity you're so obstructive,' Swanley said, smoothly.

Mrs McNaughton let the cigarette holder droop until the lighted cigarette almost touched the frilly front of her massive bosom and stared at him, her great eyes completely without expression.

'Who is the actor who uses the bats in the play?' Swanley asked.

'He doesn't use them. He simply brings them in.' Her voice was low-pitched again, and there was a trembling note in it; as of anger.

'Who is he?'

'My son.'

'Does anyone else use them?'

'No.'

'Thank you. How many people know that the bats are used as props?'

'Probably about three hundred and five,' Mrs McNaughton said with great deliberation.

Swanley gulped. 'Are you serious?'

'Perfectly. There are three hundred and twelve members of the club and the staff. To my knowledge, seven of them are confined to their homes or out of town. Others may be away. Any club member has a right to come here and could see the props. Any member can read the script, and so learn what props there are.'

'Thank you. Does your son play baseball?'

'If so, he has not confided in me.'

'Will he be here tonight?'

'Yes. Do you require anything else from me?'

'I'll be grateful if you will keep everyone out of the auditorium and away from the stage until my men have finished looking round.'

Mrs McNaughton stood up. In spite of her grotesque figure, she had a touch of dignity. In sharp contrast to her bombastic arrival, her descent of the steps was almost soundless. The door closed softly.

Swanley's smile was slightly one-sided.

'You can stay if you wish, but there's no need now, Mr Grey. You'll be in town for the next few days, I suppose?'

'I expect to be.'

'You might let me know if you're leaving, there may be

times I'd like to have a word with you,' Swanley said. 'You've been very helpful.'

'Thanks.' Tony glanced towards the door where Sarah had appeared. Was she still there? She could have crept out to the auditorium without crossing the stage, during the talk with Mrs McNaughton. He wanted to know, but it would be folly to wait, or to go to the other dressing-room. 'I think I'll go straight home.'

'Good night,' said Swanley. 'Oh – you won't forget that the most important thing is to remember if you noticed anyone else on the common. Someone hiding in the trenches, for instance, whom you may have seen without realising it. Keep at that, won't you?'

'Yes, but I'm not very hopeful.'

'Provided you try,' said Swanley. 'Discovering that a third person was there would be a great help.'

CHAPTER 7

Visitors

Without hanging about at the back of the auditorium, there was no way of finding out about Sarah. Tony walked briskly towards the door, glancing round only when he opened it. Men were coming up the stairs; Swanley's policemen, ready for their search. Swanley stood in the middle of the stage, and appeared uninterested in Sarah or anyone in the wings. Tony waited for the men to come in, the young constable who had taken him to Swanley's office, and two whom he hadn't seen before.

Then he went downstairs.

There was no sign of Sarah in the Games Room, where twenty youngsters had gathered.

'Young man!'

He stopped, and turned round.

'Yes, you.' Mrs McNaughton blocked the doorway. She had obviously been in the office, which was opposite the Games Room door. 'Come in here a minute.'

Without wanting to, indeed, longing to turn tail and run, he came.

Mrs McNaughton retreated into the office. It was large and airy, and the walls were covered with photographs – profiles, full face, head and shoulders, full length, groups and stage sets. There were several hundred of them, and one of Sarah drew his eyes as a magnet draws a pin. She was ravishing in an evening gown, gay, alluring. He made himself glance at the others, then at Mrs McNaughton. She went to her desk, and sat down heavily.

In some ways, she 'was' the club. She financed it freely,

kept the membership fees low, sparing nothing to make it a theatrical success. It was her pet, her one big interest, and because she had an autocratic mind, she ruled it absolutely.

'Sit down,' she said. 'Whisky?'

'Well – '

'*I'm* going to have one,' said Mrs McNaughton, and took a bottle of Johnnie Walker and two glasses out of a cupboard in the desk. He had heard rumours that she was a heavy drinker. Her big, gem-studded hands moved expertly, she poured out two generous tots. 'Soda?'

'Please.'

'There you are.' She pushed a glass and a syphon towards him, and drank half her own drink at a single draught, then regarded him steadily. 'You know, I've warned you against that man, Swanley. Don't make any mistake, he's dangerous.'

'He has a job to do,' Tony said.

'And he'll cause as much trouble as he can in doing it. Don't be deceived by that quiet front. He's a born actor. I feel sorry for his daughter. Know Millicent?'

'No.'

'Very neat little actress. Natural poise, too. If she had a decent father, she would be in a good Rep by now. But he has a Victorian prejudice against the theatre, which must be pandered. Aren't you a writer?'

'Well – '

'Are you or aren't you?'

'I scribble a bit.'

'Oh, modesty!' sneered Mrs McNaughton. 'Nothing worse than false modesty. Either you write or you don't. Do you?'

'Yes.'

'Tried play writing?'

'No.'

'An excellent recreation. We put on a play by one of our own members annually, if we can find one good enough. Had to miss one last year.' Mrs McNaughton's lips curled angrily at the memory. 'What makes you think you can write?'

'Optimism.'

She gave a reluctant smile.

'A splendid quality. Not of course to be confused with conceit. Tell the world you're good, and some people will come to believe it. Enjoying the club?'

'Not yet.'

'Why?'

'Well, small communities rather resent newcomers, don't they?'

'Not really, though naturally that depends. Come round and have a drink at my home on Sunday evening. I'll have a few friends there, you'll get to know them better. And don't forget I've warned you of Swanley.'

'I won't forget,' said Tony, and finished his whisky. 'Thanks for the drink.'

'A necessity,' said Mrs McNaughton. 'Those flat-footed idiots trampling all over the place, there's no telling what damage they'll do.'

Self-consciously taking his leave, Tony was acutely aware of the intentness of her gaze. He was glad when he was in the open air again. Her interest had been too sudden to be natural. He had the impression that although she disliked him, she had overcome that dislike in pursuit of some motive. He tried to stop thinking about her, succeeded for two minutes, then heard a sports car with a noisy engine, coming along the road. Beneath a street lamp, he saw the fair hair and the handsome, carefree face of the man at the wheel; it was Pat McNaughton. Close beside him, with an arm tucked through his, was a little dark-haired girl Tony didn't know.

The car roared past.

Tony turned down a side street with a cobbled surface, which he knew led to the river. The noise of the engine faded, and there were only distant sounds and, as he drew nearer, the lapping of water against the bank. A tow-path stretched right along in each direction, running through the town. On the far side, he could see a hundred lighted windows, some of them reflected on the water. Above, the night was clear and the stars looked bright and large.

There were trees on the tow-path; great chestnut trees which spread their branches wide, overhanging the river itself. There were a few cafés with gardens which stretched down to the water's edge, and many private houses backed on to the river on this side. He saw the shape of a boathouse, and the little jetty which ran out into the water.

He strolled on as far as the bridge.

His house, in Middle Street, was on the other side of the river. He walked up a flight of stone steps to the bridge and went briskly across. Soon he turned into the street – the first on the left, beyond the row of houses which, here, fronted the river. They were all large, and stood in their own grounds; most of them had private jetties and little boathouses. The Rowing Club's boathouse was half a mile away; he wanted to join the Club, but hadn't yet made inquiries about membership.

Middle Street was wide, with beech trees planted on either side, and high walls surrounding the gardens. His own house, Number 11, had six bedrooms and four reception rooms. He had already toyed with the idea of letting off part of it. There were snags, of course, and he'd have to go into that. The main thing was that the house was in good condition. Aunt Matilda hadn't believed in letting her property fall into disrepair.

He passed the shadowed figure of a policeman; then saw three or four cars parked outside Number 11. Two men stood at the gate, two others, he could just see, were on the drive.

He drew up.

The two men came quickly forward.

'Mr Grey?' one asked.

'Yes.'

'We've been waiting for you. We're from –'

'Press?' Tony asked.

One man laughed.

'You know a thing or two!'

'No more than I've told the police,' said Tony. 'Haven't you got a story from them?'

'Oh, at second-hand,' a man said. Suddenly there was a vivid flash, and a click; Tony hadn't noticed that one of the men had a camera and a flashlight. He ought to have expected it. His eyes were dazzled by the flash, and he stood quite still. 'What really happened, Mr Grey?'

'Did you see anyone?' another demanded.

'Running away, perhaps?'

'Did you try to pull him round?'

'How did you feel – did it shake you?'

There was no point in antagonising them. Tony said pleasantly:

'It's cold out here, if you really want to talk to me, why not come in?'

'Now that's what I call handsome,' the taller man said. 'Lead on, Macduff!'

They surrounded him as he walked to the front door. He took them into the drawing-room, a room he had so far rarely used, furnished in heavy, outmoded mahogany.

'Anyone like beer?'

'This man is worth knowing,' the taller reporter said 'But we don't want to rob you.'

'No robbery, I'll fix it.'

'Just a minute,' said a sharper voice. 'Let's get a few facts. You're a writer, were in the R.A.F., saw service in France, Germany, Middle East and Burma – right?'

'You're fairly accurate.'

'You inherited this house from your aunt, Matilda Henderson – any money with it?'

'Five hundred pounds.'

'A year?'

'One lump sum.'

'And you write, don't you? Books – poems – what?'

'Just a writer,' Tony said, 'and you can add the prefix "struggling". May I ask where you got all this information?'

'Oh, here and there,' said the tall man evasively. 'About the discovery – what took you out to the common?'

'Need of exercise.'

'What happened?'

He told them what he had already told Swanley. Only two of them made notes, the others seemed satisfied with memorising the information. They asked him what Swanley had said, and he shook his head, decidedly.

'You'll get me locked up.'

The tall man chuckled.

'Don't worry, we'll give you a good show. Anything else you'd like to tell us? Have you just come from the police station?'

He sensed a sharper interest, and guessed that they had tried to get him at the station, and been told that he'd left some time ago.

'No. I've been out for a stroll.' He saw no point in saying that he had been to the Theatre Club; they would probably learn that quickly enough.

'What's her name?' a man asked, and the others looked expectant.

'I've no girl friend – sorry!' He felt almost light-hearted, quite free from tension. 'I'll go and get the beer.'

'Did Swanley show you the six photographs of the luscious lovelies?'

He hadn't expected them to know that.

'As a matter of fact, he did, and each one of them was a complete stranger. Pity. I won't be half a minute.'

'Can we use the telephone?' one man asked.

'Sorry, there isn't one.'

Tony went out, whistling softly. He had put them on his side; he knew enough about the Press to be sure that they wouldn't allow personal liking to interfere with their job, but it was a good thing to have them friendly. He opened the door of the room opposite, which he had made a study-cum-living-room, groped for the light, and switched it on.

Mrs Denton was sitting there.

CHAPTER 8

Demand

She sat on an old saddle-backed chair, upright, unmoving, except that she blinked in the sudden light. Behind Tony, a man came out of the drawing-room and moved towards the front door. Tony stepped inside quickly, and closed the door behind him. He noticed that a window was open and the curtains undrawn. Walking towards them he watched the girl's pallor, her extreme immobility. He drew the curtains. Like everything else in this house, the cords worked efficiently, and the night was shut out.

He turned to face Mrs Denton.

'Did you get in through the window?'

'Yes.'

'Why?'

'I wanted to see you. The window was open, and I climbed straight in. I didn't want to walk up and down outside, I might have been seen.'

'You probably have been seen. Turn your chair round a bit, and move it further into the corner.'

She obeyed.

'I have other visitors, and if they find out you're here, you'll be on the front pages of the newspapers tomorrow morning.'

The beer was in a cupboard behind the door, and he looked inside. There were seven full and five empty half-pint bottles; that would have to be enough. He loaded them on to a tray, with five glasses, and then went to the door, balancing the tray on one hand. He didn't look at Mrs Denton again, and she didn't speak.

As the door opened, he heard the tall man say:

'He's all right.'

'Could have done it, though.'

'Two to one against him,' said a third voice.

'Don't risk your money,' Tony said, 'and come and take this, or I'll drop it.'

The tall reporter was nearest the door, and hurried forward. Tony turned out the light in the study, and closed the door with a snap. Then he remembered the bottle opener; these bottles had metal caps. He didn't want to go back, but there was only one bottle opener in the house.

'Trouble?' The tall man's nose was thin, an inquisitive nose.

He'd have to go back.

'I forgot the opener, I won't be –'

'Here,' said the reporter, and took one out of his pocket. 'I've been caught like that before. Very decent of you, Grey.'

Tony laughed. 'Swanley gave me permission to tell you anything I could, and I've no chip on my shoulder about the Press. I've nothing to fear from publicity, either. What papers do you come from?'

'Press Association,' said the tall man.

'*Express*.'

'*Mail*,' said a third.

'And its eminence, the *Daily Mirror*,' said the photographer, who had been out and now sauntered in, taking a bottle of beer as the Press Association man opened it. It bubbled up and spilled over his hand and sleeve. 'Careless brute!'

'Ever seen Denton or his wife before?' asked the *Express* reporter.

'Never.'

'Seen her since?'

'No.' Tony buried his face in his glass. 'Why should I?'

'Well, one never knows. *We* can't get at her – you might recommend your methods if you do come across her. Pretty badly cut up, wasn't she?'

'Yes, poor girl, let's not talk about her,' Tony said.

'Fair enough.'

'Oh, I don't know. Human interest and all that,' protested the *Express* man. 'We'll have to say something about her, and we may as well have it right.'

'In my opinion, she's suffering from severe shock,' Tony said. 'You can say she's nice-looking, that won't be far wrong. Brunette.'

'That'll do.' The *Daily Mail* man finished his beer, and straightened his tie. 'Thanks, Grey, we'll buzz off now, with happy memories of a Christian reception.'

The others followed him out, nodding goodbye, casual, friendly. He waited until they had reached the gate and the first car had started up, then closed the door. He didn't go into the study immediately, but stood in the hall, staring at the door. He couldn't understand why the dead man's wife had come. He remembered the fixed way in which she had stared at him, and also that he had told the reporters that he hadn't seen her. If they had any idea that she was in the house, they would make a pretty song about it.

Probably Swanley would, too.

The second and third cars started up; there had been four. He waited, and the fourth didn't move off. He went back into the drawing-room, and began to collect the bottles. With a sigh of relief he heard the engine of the fourth car starting up, then remembered the shadowed figure of the policeman. Had the man been on ordinary patrol duty, or had he been sent to watch this house? Tony went to the front door, opened it, and went to the gate. He saw the policeman, two street lamps away. The man turned smartly and walked back. Tony kept behind a gatepost, until the man reached the far corner, then turned round again.

So Swanley thought it worthwhile keeping a watch on the house, and the policeman might have seen Mrs Denton come in.

Tony went back. The door of the study was still closed. He opened it, and found the girl sitting where he had left her, her eyes still fixed in their unnatural stare. In a classic way, she was beautiful, but her pallor was alarming, and her stillness disquieting.

How should he approach her, what should he say?

At last he spoke bluntly, without subterfuge:

'Why on earth you've come here I don't know, but it's crazy. You're probably being watched by the police.'

'I wasn't followed. Even if I was – ' she shrugged. Her lips moved, her enunciation was clear, but there was no feeling in her voice. 'Where is the packet?'

Tony stared.

'Where is it?' she repeated. 'I want it, and I intend to have it.'

'I haven't the faintest idea what – '

'Please don't lie to me,' she said, flatly. 'You were the only person there, you must have taken it.'

'I tell you I haven't the faintest idea what you're talking about,' he said, and moved across to her and stood looking down. Her eyes were glassy, as if she were running a temperature. He felt suddenly very sorry for her, and all annoyance faded. 'You ought to take it easy, and – '

'I want that packet.'

'If you mean something which your husband had in his pocket, I didn't look in his pockets,' Tony said. 'Get this quite straight, Mrs Denton. I happened to be walking across the common, and found him as he was when you came up. I didn't know him, any more than I know you. If anything was taken from him, I didn't take it. It would have been crazy to touch the body – ' he checked himself, and went on quickly: 'to touch anything, as the police would soon be along.'

'You had plenty of time before anyone came,' she said. 'Why don't you admit it?'

'Because it isn't true. What was in this packet?'

She didn't answer but continued to stare at him accusingly. She wasn't convinced by his denials and in this mood, she probably would never be convinced. He pulled up a chair and sat down, trying to act normally.

'Cigarette?' he asked.

He moved about, casually looking for the box he kept for callers. This was a large room, with a high ceiling, and cream papered walls. He'd taken down all the pictures, and there were faint marks where they had been. He'd set a large oak dining-table across one corner, on which to work, and taken much of the furniture out because he liked plenty of space about him.

He found the cigarettes, gave her one and lit it. Some of the tension went out of her, but not her persistence.

She said: 'You *must* have taken it.'

'You're quite wrong, Mrs Denton.'

'I can't be.' A creeping doubt tinged her words. 'Then who could have taken it? No one else was there, or I would have seen them.'

'He'd been there for some time.'

'Not very long,' she said, and shivered suddenly. 'I don't think he'd been dead long. He – ' she broke off, as if the shivering fit were getting too much for her. Ash dropped off the cigarette and spread over her skirt, and she didn't try to brush it away.

Tony said quietly: 'You're all in, and no wonder. Like a cup of tea?'

She closed her eyes, and didn't answer.

'I'll get one,' he said.

He went out, and closed the door quietly behind him. A feeling of compassion welled up in him. If ever a girl was in need of help and consolation, it was Mrs Denton. Thoughts, speculations, crowded his mind as he went to the large, old-fashioned kitchen, which had never been properly modernised, and put on a kettle.

Had she told Swanley about the missing packet? He doubted it. How did she know that it was missing? Such knowledge was an indication that she had searched his pockets when he had gone to fetch the police. That could mean that she hadn't been so upset as she had made out. He dismissed that thought; she hadn't been acting on the common and wasn't acting now; she was overcome with grief; real grief.

He took out some biscuits, then suddenly realised that he was hungry; it was nearly nine o'clock. The girl might be hungry, too. Aunt Matilda had left a well-stocked larder. He opened a tin of ham, cut bread and butter, and loaded it on to a tray. Then he put tea in the big brown pot; the kettle was steaming fiercely. He'd been out of the front room for ten minutes or so when he went back, and wondered if she might not have gone out the way she had come; but no, there she was. She was taller than he'd thought; he was five ten, and she wasn't much less than five-six. He'd noticed her figure before, but now she moved with a supple grace which had its own peculiar attractiveness. She had long, slim legs, nicely shaped, and neat ankles. Everything about her was neat.

He put the tray down on the table, with a bang.

'Hungry?'

'You're very good.' Her voice was muffled.

'I said, hungry?'

'Not really.'

'Try some of this,' he said, and put ham on a plate, then poured out tea. 'Any friends who can come down here and keep you company?'

She said: 'No.'

'Pity.' He noted with more pleasure than he'd expected to feel, that she had begun to eat.

'Oaf! I forgot the sugar, I never take it.' He jumped up.

'Nor do I,' she said, in a high, child-like voice. 'I never – '

She couldn't go on; tears choked her. He didn't know what had caused them so suddenly, blaming himself, and wishing uncomfortably that she would stop. He remembered how Sarah Mellison had cried on his shoulder.

He heard footsteps on the gravel, and jerked his head up. Mrs Denton didn't seem to notice them, but went on crying, quietly, despairingly.

The front door bell rang.

CHAPTER 9

Gratitude

Tony moved to Mrs Denton and held her shoulders tightly; he could feel the shaking of her body.

'Mrs Denton, listen to me.'

She took no notice.

'Listen to me!' He shook her gently. 'This is urgent. It will be a bad thing for us both if you're found here. Go into the other room, and stay there until I come and see you. I've another caller.'

Obviously, she heard him, for she turned round gropingly towards the door. He took her arm and led her, still sobbing, but so quietly now, into the drawing-room. The front door bell rang again as he helped her into an armchair. Her face was still hidden, her hair falling over her hands.

'Keep very quiet. Do you understand?'

She nodded.

He went out noiselessly, closing the door. He wished he knew what he had said to make her break down.

He smoothed down his hair, and opened the front door.

Why he hadn't guessed who it was, he didn't know. He hadn't even realised that it might be a woman approaching along the drive. He stared at Sarah, standing in the porch, the light falling on her face, pin-pointing her beauty and her radiance.

She stretched out both hands, impulsively.

'You've been wonderful,' she said. 'Wonderful! I don't know how to thank you, Tony.'

He did not take her hands, but drew back, and gave a set

smile. 'Come in, Miss Mellison.' The rebuff made no difference to her, she smiled gaily and easily as she passed him, continued to smile when he led the way to the study. She glanced round.

'So this is where genius works!'

'I wouldn't know,' said Tony. 'This is where I write. What's brought you?'

'I just had to say thank you,' said Sarah, and stretched out her hands again, groping for his. She gripped them tightly, and drew nearer.

There was vitality in her, a joy of living which no one could have failed to see. Yet he did not thrill to her touch or her presence; too much had happened to offset his distant worship.

'I don't believe anyone else would have been so understanding,' Sarah said. 'You can see what it would have been like, can't you? It must have been bad enough for you. but you're a stranger, and these things are always easier for a man. Aren't they?'

'So it is said.'

She laughed. 'Well, they can't have it both ways. It was men who invented Little Helpless Women. So here I am to say thank you.' She paused. 'The rehearsal is spoiled for tonight, anyhow. The police have only just left the theatre. Everyone's bubbling over with excitement, it won't be long before they start accusing one another.'

'Did they find the other baseball bat?'

'I don't think so.' Her mood changed swiftly, became darkened, even sombre. 'To think one of those was used! I was playing with them only last night, fooling about after rehearsals. Swinging them, like Indian clubs. I may not have used the one that killed that man, but – I might have.' She went to a chair and sat on the arm, then looked at the table. The two plates and two cups and saucers told her that someone else had been there. 'Oh, Tony, I hope I haven't driven anyone away.'

He lied smoothly; he was getting good at it.

'A friend came in, but left a few minutes ago.'

'That's good,' said Sarah. 'You know, I've a feeling that I can *relax*, with you. Relax!' She slid off the arm of the chair and sat deeply in it, leaning back and closing her eyes, and stretching herself luxuriously. So she drew attention to everything that was beautiful about her. 'That's the trouble these days, one keeps on the go all the time, there's hardly any time to sit and think about things. You think a lot, don't you?'

'I brood a bit,' said Tony.

'I can tell you're a thinker,' said Sarah. 'Most of my friends are – well, like Pat McNaughton. Wonderfully good company, always gay and merry, always doing something, never happy unless they're on the move. I like it, usually, but sometimes I think it would be good to – well, just sit back and think.' She looked at the teapot, almost wistfully. 'The tea isn't hot, is it?'

'I'm afraid not,' said Tony. 'I'll make a cup, if you'd like one.'

'Oh, I would – I'm parched.'

'Rather have beer?'

'Not now,' said Sarah. 'Let me help you.' She sprang up and went to the table with speedy grace which he couldn't fail to notice. She put the things on the tray, and almost before he had reached the table, was standing with it in her hands. 'Lead on, I make a good kitchen maid.'

'You needn't – '

'I want to.'

He let her have her own way. Whatever he knew of her, there was a bewitching naturalness about her, an unforced gaiety. It was one of the things which had fascinated him, when he had seen her at the club. He'd first caught sight of her when she had been playing table tennis, with a careless ease and a poise which had made many of the club members content to sit and watch. He'd thought, then, that she was unspoiled; nothing which had since been said about her, or what she had said of herself, suggested that to be true. But the impression was strengthened by the way she behaved now.

He pushed open the kitchen door.

'My, what a dungeon!' said Sarah. 'All one wants to complete it are a few beetles.'

'Oh, it could be worse.'

'Oh, of course, so could beetles, they could be crocodiles.' She laughed, glanced round and snatched up a tea-towel. 'Tie this round my waist, will you?'

'There's no need – '

'Tie it!'

He tied it. Was it imagination, or did she lean back against him?

He put on a kettle, and stood against the big dresser, watching her. His resistance was rapidly breaking down. She looked at home there, did everything quickly and expertly. She tidied the sink and the draining board; he hadn't realised, until then, how haphazard everything was. With her quick eye and deft fingers she was magnificent. His heart missed a beat. The kettle was boiling.

He made the tea, with a slightly unsteady hand, and took biscuits from a tin.

'Do you live entirely on your own?' she asked.

'I've a woman who comes in every day for a couple of hours, that's all. And a gardener, who does some odd jobs in the house.'

'I came to a garden party here once, your aunt was always throwing garden parties for some good cause or another. I've never been one for good causes.' She seemed thoughtful. 'Perhaps that's what's wrong with me. I'm utterly thoughtless about other people. Wholly selfish.'

'I don't see why – ' he began.

She turned to him, with unexpected vigour and nearly bumped into the tray. They stood looking at each other, and he was surprised by the intensity of her gaze.

'Tony, don't say nice things. Don't flatter me. All men do. It will do me good to hear the truth, and not to be treated as if I'm a piece of useless china. Be honest with me. If you think I'm a spoiled little vixen, tell me so. Please!'

He forced a laugh.

'I will.'

'Solemnly promised?'

'Solemnly promised.'

'I'll hold you to that,' said Sarah. She laughed, unexpectedly and infectiously. 'I'll soon put it to the test, anyhow.' She led the way into the study, and closed the door after him. Then she pulled up a chair in front of the electric fire; completely at home. 'Tony, do you think I let you down badly this afternoon?'

He didn't answer.

'You promised to tell me the truth. I know that I ought to have stayed, there was no reason at all why you should lie for me. But if you really think I ought to confess to being there, I will. That's why I've come.'

'It's a bit late to tell the truth now,' he said. 'If you admit it, that will prove us both liars. And Swanley will take it for granted that we had something to hide.'

'I suppose so.' Was her expression one of relief? 'The thing is, they'd swoop on me like a pack of wolves if they thought I was mixed up in it. If you ever have a daughter, pray that her hair is straight!' She laughed, on a shrill note. 'You see, there's no false modesty about me! Perhaps none of any kind. But red hair and a fairly shapely nose can be a terrible drawback. I often wish I looked like a mouse. Without, of course, really meaning it.'

Tony stretched out for her cup.

'What's the matter?' he asked calmly. 'Sudden remorse, or did you hear what Mrs McNaughton said about you at the theatre?'

'Oh, that.' Sarah sniffed. 'That was mild. Yes, I heard. If Swanley had come in on me just then, I think I would have told him everything. No, I'm not remorseful. I'm having one of my candid moods of self-examination. I've had them before – usually when the rebuffed has turned on the rebuffer and unloaded a few home truths.' She shrugged. 'Who knows when the tables will turn? A front tooth gone, and a couple of inches changing places here and there, and hey presto!'

'Meanwhile the front tooth and the couple of inches are where they belong,' said Tony drily. He gave her more tea – and then realised that since he had opened the front door to her, he had almost forgotten that Mrs Denton was in the other room. He couldn't keep her there indefinitely, he must make sure that Sarah soon went.

'Well. I don't see that any good will come of telling Swanley the truth now.'

'You think I should have stayed with you, don't you?'

'Yes.' He was blunt.

'Why didn't you say so then?'

Tony leaned back in his chair.

'The truth, the whole truth and nothing but the truth! I was one of the hundreds of worshippers from afar. I went to Hoodle Common this afternoon because I'd been told by someone at the club that you often went there for a walk, and hoped we'd bump into each other. I know I was crazy. There it is.'

'I see,' said Sarah, slowly. 'And because I was, to you, a beautiful doll on a Christmas tree, you let me go. If I had had short legs and buck teeth you would have treated me as a responsible human being. You see what I mean about the disadvantages of beauty? Tony, don't fall in love with me. Do you hear? So many men do. There are a dozen men in Wallingham who hate the sight of me, because I've hurt their pride. Many women feel spiteful towards me, because they've seen the way their husbands and their boy friends look at me. Call it conceit, egotism, what you will, but it's true.' She paused, and then went on slowly: 'Of course, the truth is that most of the time I revel in being admired, but there are moments when these too-easy infatuations disgust me!'

She jumped up, and went to the door. She didn't look round. She was out of the house by the time he reached the hall, and although he called to her, she didn't answer.

CHAPTER 10

Problem

Seeing Mrs Denton again was like being in shadow after basking in bright sunlight. The pale-faced girl in the chair had no vitality and no radiance. She looked ill. Obviously she was not interested in his other visitor; she wasn't interested in anything.

'How are you feeling?' Tony asked.

She said evasively: 'My watch has stopped – what's the time?'

He looked at his.

'Just after nine.'

'I'll have to be going,' she said. 'A bus leaves for Hoodle at nine-thirty.'

'What about your bicycle?'

'The police are keeping it. I shouldn't feel like cycling home tonight, anyhow.'

The road from Wallingham to the village of Hoodle passed through woods, and was very lonely.

'Who will be at Hoodle to welcome you?'

'My landlady. She won't like the notoriety, but that can't be helped.'

'You could stay at a hotel there.'

'I'd rather not.' He was beginning to hate the flat monotony of her tone. 'In any case, I can't afford to stay at hotels. I doubt if I'll keep my job at Corby's after this.' Her voice was a reflection of her misery. 'Forgive me for being so depressing,' she added with a shaky laugh, her indifference suddenly pierced by a stab of social conscience. She touched her hair with blind, feminine gestures. 'I must look a wreck.'

'Stay here for half-an-hour,' Tony said suddenly. 'I want to see a man nearby, then I can take you to the bus.' He didn't wait for her answer, but added as he reached the door: 'If you miss it, we'll get a taxi.'

He'd spoken on impulse, but the arid sound of her lodgings distressed him. Asterley lived in the next street, he might suggest some happier arrangement for her.

The night struck cold.

Tony closed the front door and hurried to the street. The policeman wasn't in sight, and he couldn't hear him walking up and down. He might be standing in a doorway or a gateway, watching the house.

Seeing Asterley would probably be a good thing, would show that he had no desire to hide the fact that Mrs Denton had come to see him. Sooner or later he would have to decide what to tell the police about her visit – and her anxiety about that packet.

What did she think had been taken from her husband?

Tony walked briskly, listening for any sound of the policeman; there was none. But the feeling that he was being watched remained; he couldn't explain it. He swung round the corner, glancing back at a car that had just passed him. In the rays of the headlights he saw the furtive figure of a man, dodging back out of sight. There hadn't been time to see him clearly. But he was there, and had been watching.

Tony went on, more slowly, glanced round twice, but neither saw nor heard anything suspicious.

He turned into the next road and waited, but there was no sound. He peered round the corner, and saw no one, although there was fair light from a street lamp. It looked as if Swanley had taken the uniformed policeman away, and replaced him by a plainclothes detective.

Swanley could hardly be blamed for suspecting the man who'd found the body.

Asterley's house was the second from the corner. A red lamp outside showed the word 'Doctor' in black on the glass. There was a light in a front room. Tony rang the bell, and the door was opened almost immediately by a trim-looking maid.

'Good evening, sir.' She was foreign.

'Good evening. Is Dr Asterley in?'

'The surgery, it iss close.'

'I want to see him on a personal matter.'

'I tell heem,' she decided. 'Please to tell me your name.'

'Mr Grey.'

She drew back, and he stepped into a wide hall. The house was not unlike that in Middle Street, but the furniture was less sombre, and the atmosphere brighter and more cheerful. The maid tapped at a door, and went in.

A moment later, Asterley appeared in the doorway.

'Hallo, Grey! Want some sleeping pills? Come in.' Tony went forward into a large, delightful room of pale colours, exquisitely blended. A woman, plain but distinctive, was sitting by the fire. 'My wife,' Asterley said. 'Dora, this is young Anthony Grey, the hero of the day.'

'It's nice to see you, Mr Grey.'

Tony said: 'No hero, Mrs Asterley!' There was something pleasant about being here; a warmth and a feeling of friendliness and sincerity.

'Sit down,' said Asterley. 'I can recommend the *Drambuie*. But if you'd prefer French brandy, or whisky – '

'Thanks, but I mustn't stay,' Tony said. He didn't sit down. 'I had an unexpected visitor this evening, and she's still at my place. I'm a bit worried about her.'

'Who is she?'

'Mrs Denton.'

'Oh,' said Asterley, and frowned. 'I was a little concerned about her myself, and told Swanley so. Never a good thing, when a girl's completely alone after a shock like this. He said he was going to have her watched, in case she did anything desperate – that could happen.'

That might explain the watching man.

'She's planning to go back to her lodgings,' Tony said, 'but doesn't look quite fit enough to me. I'd suggest she stayed at my place, but I live here alone, and – '

'You keep your head out of that noose,' said Asterley promptly. 'If you take too much pity on Anne Denton, you'll find that Swanley won't believe you're strangers. Who would? It may get you into difficulties because she's come to see you, anyhow, but an all night session would be shouting for trouble. What do you want me to do?'

'If she has a sleeping draught, she'll at least be sure of a night's sleep.'

'Nice thought.'

'Rick,' Mrs Asterley broke in, 'if she's so completely alone, can't we help her?'

'My dear, I'm a police surgeon, and police surgeons can't give sanctuary to people in whom the police are professionally interested.' Asterley drummed his fingers for a moment in concentration, then leaned swiftly across for a telephone. 'Wallingham 5354 . . . Is that Mrs McNaughton?'

Tony started violently.

'Dr Asterley here,' boomed Asterley. 'I wonder if you would do a very kindly thing, Mrs McNaughton . . . '

Mrs Asterley's voice, gently insistent, overrode her husband's.

'You've had a startling introduction to Wallingham, Mr Grey, but when this is over and you've settled down, I think you'll like it. When we first came, we were sure we shouldn't want to stay when we'd been here a year, and that's fifteen years ago.'

She stopped when Asterley began to speak again; both she and Tony looked towards him.

'It's the murder business – nasty affair. The wife of the poor chap who was killed . . . Quite friendless and alone, and I'm a little worried about her . . . Well, it's been a shock she might feel desperate. Yes . . . In any case, it's bad for anyone to be left alone at a time like this, and . . . How very good of you! I'll bring her round or get young Grey to . . . You know him, don't you?'

Asterley finished talking, but not listening.

'Fine!' he boomed at last. 'In twenty minutes or so, yes. Goodbye.' He rang off, wiping imaginary sweat off his brow.

'A drastic alternative,' he said, smiling, 'but I can't think of anywhere else, except the Y.W.C.A. and I don't think that's quite what Anne Denton needs tonight. Know Mrs McNaughton, Grey?'

'We've met.' Tony was cautious.

Asterley laughed. 'I know what you mean. I'll get the car out and run Mrs Denton round to Mrs Mc's, who has some surprising qualities. The most outstanding one at the moment being her dislike of Swanley. She's been fined about fifteen times for parking her car in the wrong place at the wrong time, and regards it as a personal vendetta.'

Tony stood up. 'Don't turn out again tonight, we can walk – a walk will probably do her good.' He spoke hesitantly. 'I suppose Mrs McNaughton *is* the right person?'

Asterley shrugged. 'I'm afraid it's a case of Hobson's choice, rather than ours. She'll treat the girl fairly enough, you needn't worry about that, and she'll probably distract her from her worries. We can't expect more. You say you'd rather walk?'

'I think I would.'

'Right. The girl's alone at your place, I take it?'

'Yes.'

'I'll mix you up a sleeping draught for her, and bring it round – you go on ahead,' said Asterley.

Tony left, after less than fifteen minutes at the house, more confused than when he had gone there. Mrs McNaughton was the last person he would have thought of, and he still wasn't sure that Asterley was right; on the other hand, the doctor was probably a fair judge of human nature. The main thing was that Anne Denton wouldn't be on her own.

He walked briskly towards Middle Street, preoccupied by the realisation that he might soon have to explain Anne Denton's visit to Swanley, even tell him about the packet.

He turned the corner – and as he did so a savage punch caught him completely unaware, and sent him reeling back.

Before he could recover, his assailant came at him again. He felt a heavy blow on his head, and another across his wrist. He fell heavily, hazily aware of hands running over his body, dipping in and out of his pockets; so many hands, surely more than the two possessed by a single man.

He heard a voice mutter: 'Can't find it.'

And another in answer: 'He's got it, all right.'

A man's head bent for a second close to his face; he could just see it, through mists of pain. They had assumed that he was unconscious and harmless. He clenched his right fist – if he could punch once, in the right place, he could make them regret this. Two to one, and a groggy one at that, but it was worth trying.

A man said: 'He *must* have it.'

They had stopped searching. A pair of eyes, shadowy because of the dim street light, but eyes he would never forget, were close to Tony's.

'He's coming round.'

The man thrust out a hand and gripped Tony round the neck. His fingers were hard and the grip vice-like. Lights danced in front of Tony's eyes. He heard words which sounded like: 'Make him talk', but he couldn't be sure, his ears were throbbing too much. Then a brighter light seemed to burn his eyes, and he heard the man say:

'Look out – a car!'

CHAPTER 11

Rescue

The car drew up with a screech of brakes, while the man was still bending over Tony. He felt his head lifted, then smashed down against the pavement. He was aware of shouts, then of thuds, as if the men were running away. He gave his whole body up to pain.

He felt someone touching him. A woman said: 'He's hurt – look at his head.'

'He's breathing all right.' That was a man.

He knelt on one knee beside Tony, and felt for his pulse. Torchlight wavered over his face.

'Now take it easy,' the man said. 'Take it easy.' The phrase was soothing, anyhow. 'Try to sit up a bit.'

The woman was now on Tony's other side. Between them, they raised him to a sitting position. The man's calm voice was reassuring, in itself.

'No hurry, but tell me where you live.'

'Give him a sip of brandy,' said the woman.

'Not with a head like this. Live near here, old chap?'

'Eleven,' Tony gasped.

'Middle Street?'

'Yes – yes.' Tony tried to open his eyes, but shut them again quickly.

'That's Miss Henderson's old house,' the woman said. 'This must be her nephew. I – George!' She gasped.

'Now stop worrying,' said the man.

'But don't you remember – he found that murdered man this afternoon, everyone's talking about it! And now he's been attacked himself. How frightful!'

'Start the engine, will you?' asked George, with an obvious effort to keep things on a reasonable, non-hysterical basis.

The woman moved away. A strong arm worked itself round Tony's shoulders. Slowly, laboriously, he was helped to his feet. Swaying, he would have fallen but for the other's support.

'The car's at the kerb, it's only a step,' said the Good Samaritan. 'Take it gently.' They moved to the car. It was only a hundred yards to Number 11, and the woman drove smoothly, but even so, every movement jarred.

'Key,' said George.

With a fumbling hand Tony felt in the pocket where he kept his keys and silver.

'Gone,' he muttered. The word was like a knell of doom.

Vaguely he realised that he had left Mrs Denton in the house, and if they rang, she would probably open the door. As vaguely, he wondered whether she would feel it safer to let the caller go away. He tried to speak, but the man had gone. The woman turned to him and rested a hand on his.

'He'll manage, don't worry.'

Hazily Tony saw the shadowy figure of the man, by the window; climbing through. It was funny, somehow; everyone climbed through his window.

George came back, with the front door wide open. He didn't say anything about having seen Mrs Denton.

'All right, now, we'll soon have a doctor here. I don't see a telephone.'

'Haven't – one. Asterley's – coming.'

'Oh – good!' The man seemed surprised but satisfied. He helped Tony out, and they went slowly into the house and the study. 'Any idea how long Asterley will be?'

'Not – long.' He didn't want to talk, but to use what strength he had for thinking things out. Anne Denton. She must have heard the man break in, she –

He started up; pain streaked through his head, but didn't stop him from struggling to his feet. He saw George and the woman clearly now, for the first time. They were both plump and prosperous, and wore expressions of kindly concern touched with importance.

'Steady!' George exclaimed.

'Other – room!' gasped Tony.

He moved towards it, fighting against the pain and his weakness. He was behind George but in front of the woman when they reached the room across the hall. George flung open the door, strode in – and then stopped abruptly.

Anne Denton lay in a crumpled heap, on the floor, an ugly bruise on her temple.

Dr Asterley loomed over Tony, with a glass in his hand. He put the glass to Tony's lips. Tony took it. There wasn't much to drink, and it had a nauseating taste.

The foul draught seemed to have a miraculous effect, however.

'You'll be all right,' Asterley said. 'Nothing cracked, I'm sure of that. Bruise or two on the neck and head, that's really what it amounts to. Lucky thing the Gordons happened to come along just then.'

Tony said: 'How's – Mrs Denton?'

'Neither better nor worse than you,' said Asterley. 'I've given her an injection, she'll sleep through the night and have nothing worse than a headache in the morning.' He had been home to get the medicaments and drugs he needed, and now seemed to have time on his hands. 'I've sent for Swanley, he should be here any minute. The Gordons have gone – I said you'd say your piece to them tomorrow.'

They were in the drawing-room, Tony on a couch which had a drop-end. There was a cushion under his head, and he felt almost comfortable. The draught was working miracles; recollection had flooded back to him, sharp and vivid.

'Where's Mrs Denton?'

'In your bed – I'll arrange for a nurse to stay with her, that'll save you from awkwardness, and also save moving her. Mrs McNaughton will have to wait until tomorrow. The thing you have to remember is that worrying won't help you.'

Asterley proffered a packet of cigarettes, and took one himself. They smoked in silence for a few minutes, until a car drew up along the drive.

'I've left the front door open,' Asterley said, as they heard Swanley's heavy footsteps cross the porch. Asterley hailed him with a familiar shout. 'Here, Tom! Here!'

Swanley came in, bulky in a blue Melton overcoat, deliberate in his movements. He nodded to Tony, but didn't start to ask questions immediately. Others were with him; two men stood in the doorway, awaiting instructions.

'Sorry about this,' Swanley said at last. 'Supposing you tell me all about it? Take your time.'

The problem was knowing where to start; and Tony decided that the best place was at the point where Anne Denton had been found sitting in his study, waiting for him. He began slowly, carefully choosing his words in his anxiety not to give the wrong impression. As he talked, one of the men in the doorway made notes, while Swanley interjected an occasional word, but did not seriously interrupt.

After ten minutes, Tony leaned back.

'And that's all.'

'Did you get a clear picture of these men?'

'No. I only saw one, and didn't see him properly. I should recognise his eyes again. They seemed – ' he hesitated the only words which sprang to his mind seemed extravagant. 'Have you ever seen a vicious dog?' he said.

Swanley rubbed his chin.

'Couldn't get the colour of his eyes, or anything like that?'

'No. I had the impression of a broad nose and thick eyebrows. That's all I can say about him. He had a hoarse voice, too – though he was keeping it low.'

'His clothes?'

'I only noticed a trilby – a dark one.'

'This should be enough to help,' Swanley said, standing up. 'I think you'd better take it easy for a bit, Mr Grey. Put yourself in Dr Asterley's hands and take his advice, and you won't go far wrong. If you remember anything else, let me know.'

'Of course.'

'Hadn't seen the man before, had you?' Swanley asked, as if with a casual afterthought; but it wasn't casual, it was a deliberate trick question.

'Obviously I hadn't,' said Tony.

'Right, thanks! I'll leave a man in the house tonight, just in case this fellow wants another go at you. No idea what he was after, I suppose. He didn't say anything else?'

'No.'

'Any ideas yourself?'

'The packet Mrs Denton wanted, possibly.'

'Ah, yes,' said Swanley, as if that hadn't occurred to him. 'I'll have to speak to her in the morning. Oh, those keys – sure they're gone? You may have put them in another pocket.'

Tony felt in the others, there were no keys.

'Have you any spares?' asked Swanley.

'Yes – one of each.'

'Anything else missing?'

Tony went through his pockets again. His wallet was intact, money and papers hadn't been touched, his silver watch was still going.

'Well, that's something,' Swanley said. 'Good night.' He nodded and went out, leaving Tony to ponder on Mrs McNaughton's description of Swanley as a snake in the grass.

Tony woke up with a dull headache, and stiffness in every limb. He lay in one of the spare bedrooms, eyes narrowed, looking at the ceiling. His thoughts drifted effortlessly, airy as clouds. Daylight was coming in at the sides of the curtains; so he'd slept the night through.

The door was closed.

He pushed the bedclothes back cautiously and climbed out of bed. There was a glass of water at the side of the bed; but he wanted a cup of tea. He opened the door, and immediately a policeman appeared on the landing.

'Good morning, sir! I hope you're better.'

'Much – and I want some tea.'

'Why don't you go back to bed, sir, we can fix the tea.' The constable was the young man whom he had seen twice before – once at the police station, once at the club theatre. 'I've a colleague downstairs.'

'It suits me,' said Tony. 'Thanks.'

He went along to the large, old-fashioned bathroom. It faced east, and the light was strong at this hour of the morning, and hurt his eyes. But he looked at himself in the mirror, and grinned. There was a patch of plaster on his forehead and, when he turned his head, he could see another patch at the back. His neck was red and swollen; then he remembered the tight grip of his assailant, and also that look of fury in the smouldering eyes. He rinsed his face in cold water, then, from force of habit, went back to his own bedroom.

Anne Denton was sitting up, in his bed, looking small and forlorn in a pair of his pyjamas. She'd only just woken up, and her hair was rumpled in that charming confusion that was only allowable by women when they were alone. Then she saw him, and stiffened; and he thought that fear sprang into her mind.

CHAPTER 12
Quiet Day

He stood, neither advancing nor retreating, in the doorway, and forced a smile. The look of fear faded; perhaps she had been shocked because he looked such a wreck. He heard footsteps downstairs; the policeman was probably coming with the tea.

'Hallo,' Tony said weakly. 'Sleep well?'

'Yes – thank you.'

The policeman was coming up the stairs, and seemed to be hurrying, in spite of the tray in his hands.

'Mr Grey!' The policeman's voice held an anxious note. 'Don't disturb the young lady. I've had orders – '

'She's awake.'

'That's good,' said the policeman, in the hearty voice of a deceiver, 'but the *doctor* said she wasn't to talk to anyone when she came round, he must see her before she's allowed to talk.' He looked agitated.

'Well, well, I'll be seeing you,' Tony said.

There was nothing he could usefully say to the girl. She didn't smile as he went out, followed closely by the young constable.

'Why not get back into bed, sir, I'm sure you – '

'This chair's all right.' Tony sank into it, and reached for the tea. It was hot and stronger than he liked it; but it did him good.

He'd no doubt that Swanley would soon be here, to talk to the girl.

Swanley arrived half-an-hour later; it was then ten minutes

past nine. Tony heard his footsteps mounting the stairs. Then a door closed. He was with the girl for about half-an-hour, and Tony, wishing that he'd taken the policeman's advice and gone back to bed, sat in the chair and smoked a cigarette.

Swanley tapped at last, and came in.

'Good morning, Mr Grey – you're looking better.'

'I'll do,' said Tony briefly. 'How's Mrs Denton?'

'Nothing serious, as far as I can see. I think Dr Asterley will look in in the morning, and he'll probably say that it's all right for her to leave. Have you anything else to tell me?'

'Nothing, I'm afraid. Believe me, I'm as keen as you are to get my hands on that beggar who attacked me last night.'

'We'll get him,' Swanley said. He went across to the bed, and sat down. 'Mr Grey, you don't need telling that this is an extremely grave case. Murder and attempted murder, and there's no certainty that we've seen the end of it.'

Tony said drily: 'It had occurred to me.'

Choosing his words with great care, Swanley went on earnestly: 'It may be that you know something which would help us but that, for some special reason, you prefer to keep secret. Something which in no way involves you personally in the actual crime.'

'Well?' Tony was abrupt.

'My strong advice is that you tell us everything, Mr Grey. It could be unpleasant for you if we discovered that you'd been telling only part of the truth. It might also prevent us from finding the murderer in time to prevent other crimes.'

'There's nothing else I know that could be of use to you.' But there was Sarah; and he could picture her, wildly angry as she had been when standing over Denton's body, then radiant as she had appeared last night, again sober, almost sombre, during that unexpected period of self analysis.

Swanley said: 'Very well. But remember that murder is more serious than any other crime. Remember, too, that I am not greatly interested in anything you or anyone else may have done in the past, all I want is the truth about what has happened now. If you have any influence with anyone, tell them that.'

'I have none, but why don't you say whom you mean?'

'I mean your friend Mrs Denton,' Swanley said, as he stood up.

'But she's not –'

Swanley shrugged his shoulders, and went out without another word.

That was the only unpleasant incident in a quiet morning. Tony dressed in time for a cold lunch, prepared by his daily help, an unimaginative middle-aged woman more excited than shocked by what had happened. A policeman stayed on the premises, all day. After lunch, Asterley took Anne Denton away – presumably to Mrs McNaughton. Tony had seen her twice, for a few minutes, but they had had nothing much to say to each other.

The newspapers were full of the case. Side by side with his photograph appeared one of Anne Denton, smiling happily as she stood beside her husband on a stretch of sun-bleached sand. Less prominently, but perhaps more significantly, were photographs of the six girls whose pictures Swanley had shown him, and the caption: *The police would like to interview each of these women, believed to be friends of the murdered man.*

The implications were obvious, but did not necessarily prove that Ray Denton had been a gay Lothario. Swanley might have heard from one or more of them, by now, but Swanley probably wouldn't pass the news on; he would release only what he wanted known.

Tony was gradually getting used to the fact that he, himself, was under suspicion.

Two more reporters called to see him. Asterley looked in during the afternoon, bringing a bunch of grapes.

'From Dora – she always has a soft spot for young men with a cleft in their chin!'

Mrs McNaughton sent a brief note, hoping that he would soon recover and assuring him that she would do all she could to help Mrs Denton. It was odd that Asterley had thought of her home as a sanctuary for Anne. An exhausting woman, he thought, even for those untouched by worry or grief. Well, there was nothing he could do about it.

He didn't hear from Sarah. That surprised him, after the good impression she had set out to make last night. He wondered if she regretted her candour; then whether she had simply set out to make a fool of him, and to find out if he were going to keep the bargain. After all, she was a good actress; Mrs McNaughton had conceded that, and Mrs McNaughton was a fair judge.

Why should she be so anxious to be kept out of the affair?

Was it just because she would become the butt of every malicious tongue in Wallingham?

There was another reason. Sarah could have killed the man; she'd had access to the weapon and had been on the scene. After killing Denton, she might have started to hurry away, seen Tony, and decided to come back and brazen it out. She had come from the direction of the trenches –

It was only now he realised that she could have gone there to hide the baseball bat.

She'd been calm enough at first, then flown into a temper, and started accusing him. It could have been an act. He was crazy to keep the truth from the police, but – supposing he told them? What would happen?

Arrest?

Well, they hadn't arrested him. Suspicion? If she hadn't committed the murder, suspicion wouldn't matter, and this added evidence might help the police to find out who had.

She might, though, be implicated. Someone else might have been hiding in the trench.

Why had she chosen that particular walk? She often took it, if his information was right, but she didn't give the impression of a girl who walked for the sake of walking; such a habit was out of character. But if she had an assignation on the common, that would show everything up in a new, and ugly, light.

Judged by the evidence of the photographs, Denton had been attractive to women. Sarah had a bad reputation with men and hadn't tried to hide it, probably because she knew that he would hear the gossips talking. On her own admission, some men hated her, because she had trifled with them. Supposing she had played the fool with Denton, and he had reacted violently?

Face it. With, or without, an accomplice, she could undoubtedly have killed Denton. Swanley would not be able to tell whether she or Tony was more likely; but he, Anthony Grey, knowing his own innocence, had the best possible reason for suspecting Sarah.

He sat in the study, brooding over the whole affair. He knew that only a fool would keep quiet any longer. Swanley had warned him plainly, and the warning shouldn't have been necessary. There was only one excuse for keeping silent; to protect Sarah.

Why?

He'd believed himself to be in love with her. He'd certainly been infatuated, fascinated by her radiance, her vitality, her lovely body and her beautiful face. If he'd known her for years, he might be justified in this form of protection, but not now – especially after he'd heard so much about her. He'd given her his word, but there were occasions when it was more honourable to break a promise than to keep it. Was this one of them?

He heard a car come into the drive, went to the front door, and admitted Asterley.

'Hallo, Tony. Had a good meal today? Ah, I thought not. Now don't argue, you're coming to have dinner with me. Dora insists.'

'It's extremely good of you, but –'

'And the tweed jacket is perfectly all right,' said Asterley. 'You may brush your hair.' He seemed younger and more buoyant, and – like an old friend. Any suspicion that he was really working as an *agent provocateur* for Swanley had faded. 'I'll give you five minutes.'

Tony laughed.

'All right. It's your own responsibility if I make noises over soup.'

'No soup,' said Asterley gravely. 'We study our guests.'

Tony, taking rather less than the allotted five minutes, thought only of one thing. If he confided in Asterley without mentioning names, he could at least have someone's judgement to support his own. He decided to talk.

Coming back to the room, he put his hand tentatively on Asterley's arm.

'Before we go,' he said awkwardly, 'I'd like your advice.'

'Gladly.' Asterley dropped back into his chair again.

Now that he was at the point of it, Tony found it more difficult than he had expected. Was it betrayal if Sarah were guilty – ?

'Fire away,' said Asterley. 'It's about the Dentons, isn't it? It's been pretty obvious from the beginning that you knew them. But anything you care to tell me is, of course, confidential, unless you say the word.'

He was smiling, but serious.

CHAPTER 13

Dinner For Four

Tony stared down at the police-surgeon, who lay back in his favourite position, legs stretched out revealing his great length.

'Knowing the Dentons doesn't make one a murderer or a criminal,' he said. 'But in any case, you're wrong, Asterley.'

'Eh?'

'You're wrong, and Swanley's wrong. Until yesterday afternoon, I'd never set eyes on a Denton. I didn't know the Dentons existed. If this is the way Swanley is building up his case, he's going to have some demolition work to do.' He laughed. 'For a minute, you had me scared!'

'Hum,' said Asterley, heavily. 'For a moment, you almost had me convinced.'

Tony took out his pipe and began to fill it.

'If I can't make you believe me, I can't; but it's the truth. What makes you doubt it?'

'Anne Denton coming here. The fact that you met on the common. The fact that she thinks you have something belonging to her. The evidence that others think the same, and nearly killed you while trying to find it.'

'One mistake built up upon another,' said Tony.

'Hum.' Asterley looked at him speculatively. 'I'm much more inclined to believe you than I was. But I'm sure of this; you've a guilty secret, Tony. You are not of the stuff of which good liars are made. Swanley and I are both fairly used to judging people. You've been hiding something. What is it?'

Tony lit his pipe; it began to draw well. Asterley's

friendly use of his christian name warmed him.

'There was someone else on the common. A woman. I saw and talked to her.'

'*Another* woman?'

'Yes. An – acquaintance.' Tony shrugged, finding this easier than he'd expected. 'I've no friends here, you know, so that might mean anyone. I'm not telling you her name yet, I'm just asking for a considered opinion. I don't want to get her mixed up in it, if it can be avoided. She'd be the butt of gossip and scandal. I've no reason to believe that she knew Denton, or killed him.'

'I see,' said Asterley, heavily.

'That's everything,' Tony said.

'Not everything, old chap. Not everything by a long chalk. You've forgotten to tell me what a congenital idiot you are. How could I guess? Put your head in a noose by all means. After all, acquaintanceship is sacred. Let the little lady get away with murder. It's a form of murder, even if she didn't kill Denton. She's murdering your chances of convincing the police that you were an innocent passer-by. Oh, don't tell Swanley. Hug it to yourself. Of course, you could always spring it as a surprise as you're marched into your cell to commence a life sentence. They might listen. On the other hand, they might not.' He stood up. 'Tony, you're the worst kind of ass, a romantic one.'

Tony laughed.

'You've almost convinced me,' he said drily.

'I strongly advise you to get the process completed before the night's out. Someone's head is going to roll for this, and I would rather it was not yours. But we're late, I promised to have you on the doorstep by eight o'clock, the women are –'

He broke off abruptly, and stared at Tony with eyes both sharp and shrewd.

'Got it!' he exclaimed. 'The besom!'

'I suppose you know what you're talking about.'

'Oh, *I* know. Let's find out if you do.' Asterley chuckled. 'Come on.'

It was a fine, clear night. An aeroplane droned overhead, a somnolent background to the hum of traffic. A policeman walked past on the other side of the road, as the car nosed its way out of the drive. So there was a watch inside and outside the house. The full significance of that couldn't be missed. On the excuse of making sure that he wasn't attacked again, Swanley was keeping him under close surveillance. Tony had no one to blame for that, but himself. He'd taken Asterley's sarcasm lightly, but he was beginning to see the sense behind it.

Asterley pulled up outside his house, opened the front door with a key, and stepped within, calling:

'Eight o'clock precisely!'

They moved towards the sitting-room. Mrs Asterley was standing by the fire smiling at him, and Sarah stood beside her.

Asterley had guessed the truth, of course; Sarah must have asked to meet Tony here, Asterley had arranged it – and the reason for the request had been obvious as soon as he had heard Tony's story. There was nothing in Asterley's manner to give that or anything else away.

'Here we are, then! Tony, you've met Sarah Mellison, haven't you?'

'Of course, we've met.' Sarah beamed at them. 'We're club members.'

'How are you?' Tony tried to sound enthusiastic. 'Good evening, Mrs Asterley. It's extremely kind of you to take pity on me, and –'

'Give him a drink and keep him quiet,' Asterley said. 'Sarah, I must say it, you're looking more superlatively beautiful than ever. Isn't she, Dora?'

'What can any jealous wife answer to that!' Mrs Asterley said, laughing.

'Isn't it wonderful to see such a perfectly happy couple, Mr Grey?' Sarah murmured.

'Mr Grey'; nothing to suggest the warmth of 'Tony' as she'd uttered it last night; nothing to suggest that they were anything more than club acquaintances.

'Marvellous,' Tony said dryly.

'This smart talk,' complained Asterley, 'and we ought to be discussing the state of the world or the latest betting on the Two Thousand Guineas. Do much betting, Tony?'

'Five shillings each way on the big races, if I remember in time,' Tony said.

'Sound policy.' Asterley took a whisky and soda from his wife and passed it to Tony. 'Or else we ought to be discussing Wallingham's great sensation. The first murder in the police district for twenty-seven years. No wonder Swanley is setting his teeth grimly and determined at all costs to see it through. Able chap. Last thing he wants, I imagine, is to call in Scotland Yard, but he'll probably have to, before it's finished.'

'Scotland Yard!' exclaimed Sarah.

'It has got rather a quelling sound, hasn't it? Very bright men, though.'

'Rick,' interrupted his wife, 'ought you to talk about the murder? It isn't the best of social topics, and you are a police-surgeon.'

'Sworn only to secrecy on matters of particular interest, which in no way bars me from taking part in a general discussion. Murder is the subject over practically every dinner table in the town tonight, at every pub, every café. Why not? We're a sensation-loving people. Incidentally, Swanley did a smart job in keeping the news of the attack on Tony and Mrs Denton out of the newspapers.'

'How *is* your head?' asked Sarah, her voice filled with the social concern of a woman who couldn't care less.

The telephone bell rang.

'No, I will not go out again until after dinner,' Asterley said firmly. 'I'll take it in the surgery, my dear.' He went out, and Mrs Asterley moved after him.

'Sarah, look after Mr Grey for a few minutes, I must have a word with Cook.' She followed her husband, and closed the door.

Sarah was now standing by the fire. She didn't move,

didn't hold out her hands, but looked at Tony with such intensity that he felt his resistance melting; that was the trouble, when she was near he couldn't be dispassionate. He thrust his hands in his pockets, and forced a smile.

'Strange coincidence,' he said.

'Coincidence!' echoed Sarah, and she had never looked more radiant. 'I fixed it, Tony! We can meet as often as we like after this, without giving Swanley cause for the slightest suspicion!'

'I see,' said Tony.

'What's the matter?' Sarah asked.

'I'm wondering where tricks and subterfuge are going to land us,' Tony said.

'You mean – you're regretting it?'

'I am.'

The radiance faded from her eyes, and a frown replaced it.

'Wasn't that our bargain – the simple truth?' he asked.

'Simple? Is that what you call it?' Sarah's eyes flashed. She looked even more beautiful as her temper rose. 'Why didn't you say this last night?'

'I said, if you remember, that I couldn't see any good would come of telling Swanley the truth now, it would only look bad for both of us. That didn't stop me from regretting that I'd been fool enough to let you go.'

A storm was gathering in her eyes; she reminded him of the way she had looked on the common.

'I'm disappointed in you,' she said abruptly.

'People never come up to our expectations, do they?' Tony asked.

She turned and took a cigarette off the mantelpiece, lit it from a table lighter. Her hand wasn't very steady. This was worse than he had expected. He tried to divert his thoughts but couldn't take his gaze away from her. Whatever she had done, whatever she was planning, she was a most desirable creature. Creature! She was the loveliest thing he had ever seen.

He relaxed.

'Sarah, it's going to be a bad few days, but when it's cleared up, we can get on a better footing.'

'When it's cleared up,' said Sarah icily, 'we are unlikely to be on any footing at all.' She moved round abruptly, turning up the volume of the radio.

Asterley came in, breezily.

'How the young love noise. Sarah, do pander to my declining years and turn it low again. I came to tell you that dinner's ready.'

She was quite unpredictable. She switched the radio down, moved to Tony's side and slipped her arm through his. Asterley led the way across the hall into the dining-room. This was a graceful room, lit by candles. The Asterleys sat at each end of the long, rosewood table. Sarah and Tony sat opposite each other.

Sarah could not have been more gay.

There was smoked salmon, roast duck and green peas, a soufflé that would have done credit to a Paris chef. The air of intimacy gradually broke down Tony's resistance. Thoughts of murder and suspicion faded, this was Tony's first real intimation of the possible delights of Wallingham.

'Port?' Asterley asked, while they were waiting for coffee. 'Sarah?'

'Yes, please.'

Asterley poured the wine. He was smiling.

'Do you mind telling me why you really wanted to meet Tony?'

CHAPTER 14

Angry Sarah

Mrs Asterley wasn't surprised. Tony was looking at her as her husband spoke, and saw the faint smile which curved her lips. She turned from Tony to Sarah. They all looked at Sarah. She had been smiling too, but now the smile was gone. She withdrew her hand from her glass, and stared at Asterley; and there was no friendliness in her expression.

'I don't understand you,' she said.

'You do, you know. I am all kinds of a fool, of course, but I know Sarah Mellison fairly well. I know that while she relishes sensation, she is also fastidious. Half of Wallingham is convinced that Tony killed this man. Think what spending a convivial evening with him would do to your reputation! You overplayed your hand, my dear.'

'You are talking nonsense.' Sarah's voice was icy.

'Oh, I don't think so. Port, Tony?'

'Thanks.'

'I'd rather not continue with this discussion,' Sarah said.

'But I think we should, Sarah.' Asterley dropped the flippant tone, and leaned across the table, towards her. 'Be sensible about it. I am officially connected with the police, but it's no part of my job to involve people, only to advise them to do the wise thing. Tony, in the greatest of good faith, told me that there was someone else on the common. He didn't say it was a pretty woman, but that was fairly obvious. You were most anxious to meet him. What's more, you called on him last night, one of Swanley's men told me that. I knew you were looking for an excuse to meet him again and become well acquainted. I wondered why. Were you on the common, Sarah?'

As he had talked, colour had first fled from, and then flushed, her cheeks. Her eyes glittered, she had never looked more angry. She played with the stem of her wine glass, gripping it so tightly that it looked as if she might break it.

Mrs Asterley watched her closely.

'Well?' Asterley said, quietly.

'You have no right to talk like this.'

'But I have. A life's at stake. He doesn't seem to realise it yet, but the most likely one is Tony's.'

'How would it help Tony if mine were added to the list?'

Asterley stood up and moved towards her, then put a hand on her shoulder. She stared straight ahead; not at, but through, Tony.

'Did you kill Denton, Sarah?'

She flung his hand off, pushed her chair back, and ran out of the room. Her footsteps, sharp and staccato, crossed the hall floor. The front door opened.

'Go after her, Rick,' Mrs Asterley urged.

'I wonder if I should,' said Asterley. 'I thought she had more in her than this.' He stared at the door. 'Anyhow, it will probably do her good. She'll realise that Swanley will have to know. Pity, but – ' he shrugged. 'Don't blame yourself, Tony, you did more than you should have done.'

Tony said: 'Perhaps. But I can't leave her like this.'

He stood up, looked towards Mrs Asterley with an expression that both asked for permission, and tendered an apology, and went out. The front door was wide open; Sarah's footsteps were just audible. When he reached the gate, he could hear her walking towards the main road and the river. He ran after her, making little sound. He didn't know or care whether Asterley was following.

She was over the bridge and close to the steps leading to the tow-path, when at last he drew up with her. He was breathing hard, and his head was beginning to throb.

'Sarah.'

She started, glanced round, and then looked away again.

The light wasn't good enough now for him to see her eyes; but he could imagine the anger still in them.

'Sarah, I'm dreadfully sorry about all this.'

She said : 'I don't want to talk about it, least of all to you.'

'I didn't tell him.'

'I don't believe you.'

'I can't help that, I didn't tell him. Damn it, doesn't it mean anything to you that I've risked my neck to keep you out of it?'

They reached the steps, and Sarah hesitated. She had no coat on; she shivered.

'You'd better get home,' Tony said gruffly. He looked round, half-expecting to see Asterley, but the doctor wasn't in sight. 'Come on.'

A tall broad man whom he thought he recognised was halfway across the bridge leaning over and looking into the river; it was almost certainly one of Swanley's men. Until tonight, he hadn't realised that he was under such extreme suspicion. How absurdly trusting he had been! It was as if the normal power of reasoning and calculating had left him since he had found the body of the dead man, and quarrelled with Sarah.

'I'm not going home yet,' Sarah said, and turned down the steps, abruptly.

He knew that she expected him to follow. He glanced round at the man on the parapet, and saw that he was looking their way. Did it matter? Swanley would be told about this, would almost certainly question Sarah. Asterley could hardly keep back the information that he'd gained. There was no way, now, of keeping Sarah's name out of it.

He followed her, hurrying along the tow-path, and soon they were walking side by side. He could hear her breathing, and her teeth beginning to chatter. There was only one thing to do. He did it with a feeling of resentment; it shouldn't have been necessary. She had a way of making him do unnecessary and damaging things.

He put the things out of his coat into his trouser pockets, took the coat off, and draped it round her shoulders. She didn't speak, but clutched it in front of her. They continued to walk briskly, passing the little jetty which he had seen the previous night. At this rate they would soon reach the alley which led to the theatre. He didn't know where she lived, but believed it was on the outskirts of the town, on this side of the river. He knew little about her family, but her clothes, and way of life, indicated no shortage of money.

They crossed the end of the jetty.

There was no sound behind them, and there would have been, had anyone been following. Swanley's man was probably sure they were heading for the theatre club, and would be waiting for them there.

The silence between them began to get on his nerves.

'Must you sulk?' he asked abruptly.

'I've nothing to say.'

'Well, I've plenty. Sooner or later, this had to come out. We ought to have known that. By behaving like a hysterical schoolgirl, you practically told Asterley that you've something to hide. He'll have to tell Swanley.'

'Well, that's what you wanted, isn't it?'

'Don't be a fool! It was your fault, if you hadn't schemed to be at that dinner tonight, he would never have guessed whom I meant.'

'You'd have found a way to tell him,' Sarah said tensely. 'You would probably have said that it was just a hysterical schoolgirl, and he would have known in a moment who it was.' Her tongue could be like a lash. 'I'm beginning to understand why you let me leave you on the common.'

'Then you know more than I do.'

'Do I?' They were staring straight ahead of them, and he felt a quickening anger. 'I know this, Mr Grey. That you killed that man, and when I came along, you saw a golden opportunity to involve *me*. You encouraged me to go, meaning to tell everyone that I'd been there. That would allow you to pose as a gallant hero, and make everyone think that I had something to hide. Oh, it's brilliantly clever. I didn't realise you were so good.'

He flashed: 'You're unbearable! After I've done my damnedest – '

'To get *me* involved.'

He raised his voice. 'I tell you I've risked my own neck! If I'd had any idea what kind of idiot you are, I wouldn't have chanced it. Haven't you any sense? Or are you just a lovely shell, without a mind, heart or ounce of decent feeling in you? You're behaving like a spoiled brat, and it's time someone took you in hand.'

There was silence but for those small, sucking waves, lapping against the bank. They had passed the alley which led to the theatre, and here fields came down almost to the water's edge.

'Please go,' she said in a taut voice.

'Not yet. You'll fall into the river and then blame me for pushing you, if I leave you here.'

'Then you might at least keep quiet.'

They walked another hundred yards in silence, their footsteps making practically no sound. Faint strains of music drifted across the water.

He began to feel cold. This was insanity. They were behaving like children. All the sound sense of maturity had been drained out of them. He stretched out a hand, to touch her shoulder, withdrew it sharply, and said in a low-pitched voice:

'Sarah, we've got to pull ourselves together. The fact is, we're both in a jam. It won't do any good blaming each other for it. If we quarrel, we'll only make the mess worse. We've got to find an agreed way of telling Swanley, and making it look as good as we can. If I've judged Asterley properly, he'll give us the chance of telling Swanley ourselves. The wise thing would be for you to tell him.'

'Oh, yes – leave the foulest part of the job to me.' She seemed to hiss the words.

'I'm trying to think of the best thing for you,' he persisted, and touched her arm. She shook off his hand, as vigorously as she had shaken off Asterley's. He felt himself tightening up inside, the fire of anger which he'd managed to damp down would flare up again if they went on like this. 'Sarah, once and for all, are you going to make matters worse by behaving as if you're as guilty as hell? I shall soon start believing that you did kill Denton.'

She caught her breath, and swung round on him. There was only the startlight; and he could only see her face in outline. She actually struck at him, as she cried:

'Get away from me! I don't like talking to a murderer. Get away!'

He swung on his heel, flaming with anger – and as he did so, a shadowy figure leapt out of the darkness, grabbed him by the shoulders and flung him back, against Sarah. He didn't see what happened, just felt the hand at his shoulders gripping, thrusting, clawing, and then a terrific punch in the stomach.

Somewhere, above Sarah's scream, a voice rasped:

'I'll smash your face in if you don't give me that –'

There was another scream; and a splash. The man's grip relaxed. Tony felt himself slipping over the bank, tried to recover, and pitched into the icy water.

CHAPTER 15

Cold Water

Tony felt the water closing over his head, and its coldness shocked him. He went down, gulped, took in a mouthful of water, and began to strike out blindly. Something clutched at his right hand, and he went under again.

Realising the danger of near-panic, he tried to slacken his threshing limbs. Ordered, disciplined, he felt himself floating to the surface. He took in a great gulp of air, retched, and was sick. He struck out, slowly, deliberately. Something clutched at him, pulling at his legs.

Weeds.

Cold dread struck at him; colder than the water itself. The threat of panic came again. He fought it back – and then his right foot touched bottom. He drew his left leg along, soon he was standing upright, with his chin just above water.

The weeds swayed gently against him; there was a bed of them here, thick as grass.

He heard splashing. Straining to hear, to see, he shouted:

'Sarah!'

Only the sound of splashing came back – no cry, no gasp, nothing to suggest that she could hear him. The noise was a few yards away, on his right – farther away from the river bank. The only light was the reflection of the stars themselves – they were dancing about wildly in the disturbed water, not far ahead of him. Sarah was there, drowning, caught by the weeds.

'Sarah!'

There was despair in his voice. He moved forward, his

hands outstretched. Suddenly he was out of his depth, the bed of the river dipping steeply. He went under, came up again, gasping, then he saw what he wanted most; a light. It came from the bank, a steady beam sweeping in wide half-circles. A man's voice called out:

'Where are you?'

'This way!' yelled Tony. The light swivelled towards him, and caught his face. 'Straight on!' The light passed him, a bright orb and a powerful beam. It shone upon smooth water – and upon Sarah's hair, floating on the surface.

He plunged forward, losing sight of the hair for a moment, then seeing it again. He was only a couple of yards away. Two strokes, and he was able to touch it. Everything he had learned about life-saving came to his mind; it was pitifully little. But he kept himself afloat with his left hand, and groped for her shoulders. He touched her face. The silence was frightening. He moved his hand, and managed to put it behind her shoulder, and raise her slightly. She was a dead weight, but the light on the river bank kept steady, and he could see her face. He had to make sure that she was floating on her back, then turn on his back, hold her head between his hands and swim towards the bank, using only his legs.

There seemed to be no weeds here.

'How are you doing?' The man's words echoed clearly across the water.

'Hold it steady.'

Tony hardly knew how he managed the task. It was no more than fifteen or twenty feet, but seemed miles. He felt weeds clutching at his legs again, and the long tendrils sweeping his face; one slithered across his mouth, and he retched, and almost let Sarah go. A moment later, his head touched the bank. He let his legs drop and found that he was within his depth.

The light was now lower, the lamp standing on the bank itself. A man said from above his head:

'Can you raise her?'

'Just – a – minute.' He was gasping for breath, but at least they were both out of danger. She hadn't been under long enough to drown; it was unthinkable. He gripped Sarah round the waist, and said: 'Ready.'

'Just get her up a few inches.'

Tony saw the man crouching on the bank, hands stretched downwards. Sarah seemed to weigh a ton. The man groped, just touching her. Tony hoisted her again in a supreme effort. This time the man was able to clutch her arms, dragging her over the bank.

Tony scrambled out after her, falling forward on to the hard ground, breathing in loud, gasping sobs, his head throbbing wildly.

Gradually the pain subsided and he struggled up, first to his hands and knees, and then, rather staggeringly, to his feet. As he did so, the torch wavered violently.

'Good Lord!' the man exclaimed. 'It's Sarah Mellison!' He turned it on Tony. 'What the devil was she –'

'Never mind that!' Tony gasped. 'She needs artificial respiration, we've got to get busy.'

'Hell of a place for that,' the man said. There was something vaguely familiar in his voice. 'Look here, she only lives ten minutes away. If we could get her there, it would be much simpler.'

'Don't be a fool, minutes count.'

He watched the other turn Sarah on to her stomach, then kneel astride her. He ached to help, and moved forward, picking up the lamp. Water trickled from her mouth. The man was gasping for breath, and Tony said:

'Let me have a go.'

'No, I can –'

Tony cried: 'She's breathing!'

Five minutes later, she was breathing evenly and regularly.

'Come on, hold the bike up,' said the stranger. 'I'll get her on to the saddle. It's not ten minutes, we'll be there in no time.' Together they hoisted the girl's inert, dead weight. 'I'll lead the way,' the man continued.

He pushed the bicycle towards the side of the towing path, somehow contriving to fit the lamp over its socket and support Sarah. Not far off, lights showed at windows, pale yellow squares, suggesting quiet and comfort and safety.

It was an age; ten minutes was a ridiculous underestimate. But there was nothing else to do, and the stranger was calm and competent. Why did his voice sound familiar? That was something to think about, and Tony forced his thoughts on to it. It was a rather deep voice with a curious lilt; where had he heard it before?

They passed the gate of a house.

'Let's take her there,' Tony said.

'Only two more houses, old chap. You go ahead – it's that white house.' There was a light over the door, bright against the pale walls. 'We can take her straight in.'

Tony went forward, unsteadily. His head was hammering, his feet wouldn't go where he wanted, but he reached the drive some way ahead of the other, and was at the front door when the bicycle turned in at the gates. He put his finger on the bell and kept it there, not knowing what to expect. There was a ready answer, and a young maid, in a neat housedress, opened the door.

She screamed: 'Oh!' at sight of him, and backed away, hands held high in fright.

'What's this?' A man appeared from a room on the right – the tall, familiar, welcome figure of Rick Asterley.

Asterley and the maid were upstairs, with Sarah; they had been up there for twenty minutes; or an hour. Tony, wearing a pair of borrowed pyjamas and a thick woollen dressing-gown, sat with a whisky and soda by his side, in front of an electric fire; he felt too hot. The cyclist was sitting on a piano stool; they were in the drawing room of a modern, well-to-do house, the furniture a pale, creamy brown, the walls hung with pictures both brilliant in colour and, to the layman's eye, clumsy in execution.

The cyclist was a tall, dark-haired man of about thirty, with a strong face, good, clear brown eyes, a mouth that was ready to smile. They had met before; he was Jim Norton, one of the players in the cast of the American play being rehearsed at the club.

'I was just coming away,' he said, for the second time. 'Sarah didn't turn up, the rehearsal was a flop, Mrs Mac was in a fine old tantrum. We packed up early. I live a bit farther along the river. I always cycle along that path. Good thing I do.'

'Very.'

Tony looked at the door; the minutes were creeping on towards twenty-five. There was no sound from above, no indication of what was happening.

'She'll be all right,' Norton said. 'She couldn't have been under for more than three minutes. I hope she appreciates what you did, Grey.'

'I don't see that it matters.'

Norton smiled; he was much more attractive when he smiled.

'However you put it, you saved her life.'

Tony shrugged. 'I doubt if I could have got her on to the bank alone. Did you see anyone else?'

'I did and I didn't.' Norton put down his glass appreciatively. 'I was halfway between the club and the spot where I found you, when I heard a woman cry out. I thought a Romeo was going too far! Often hear virtuous protests when I'm cycling along, what the little idiots think that they're brought out there for, I don't know. I heard a splash, and then a chap ran hell-for-leather past me. I didn't see him closely, and thought I'd be more useful worrying about whoever was having a ducking. Cigarette?'

'Thanks.'

Tony accepted a light, and looked at the door again.

'You can never hurry Asterley,' the other said comfortably. 'I wonder what he was doing here.'

Tony had a pretty shrewd idea. Asterley had come to see Sarah, decided to wait for her, and so had been in exactly the right place at the right moment.

'Come to that,' went on Norton casually, 'you're a pretty

fast worker, aren't you? Walking along the tow-path with the glamorous Sarah, when you hardly know her. There's one quarter where she won't be very popular, though. She's an actress in ten thousand, but after tonight, Mrs McNaughton will be out for her blood I'm afraid. To cut a rehearsal without giving warning is, to her, the one unforgivable sin.'

Tony said: 'We'd been out to dinner, and walked back that way.'

'No business of mine,' Norton said, 'but since you're so much in the news, I couldn't help wondering. Any sign of the murderer, yet?'

'Wasn't that one tonight?' asked Tony, and could have cut his tongue out.

Norton drained his glass, and put it down on the mantelpiece.

'Just what happened?'

'He was after something he thinks I have. Whether he meant to tip us in the river I don't know.'

He would have to tell Swanley soon, ought to be at the telephone now, but he couldn't concentrate on anything until he knew the report on Sarah. He stood up, abruptly. Half-an-hour had passed since she'd been taken upstairs, it might be serious trouble. He went to the door, knowing that Norton was watching him intently, that he was giving his feelings away.

There was a light on in the square hall, another on the landing above.

Then a door opened upstairs, and a long shadow appeared.

CHAPTER 16

Unsolicited Gift

Tony stood at the foot of the stairs as Asterley started down, and his voice was harsh.

'Well?'

'All's well,' Asterley said, comfortably. 'She'll be all right. She's conscious, feeling a bit down, but there's no danger now. What happened?'

'We were pushed in, and –'

'Grey pulled her out,' Norton chanted magnanimously, from the drawing-room door.

'Any idea who it was?'

'No – someone jumped at us from the towing path. I hadn't any idea he was there.'

'Rushed past me, a few minutes afterwards,' said Norton. 'Well, well, if Sarah's all right, I'll be pushing along.'

'I should stay a bit longer,' advised Asterley. 'I must telephone for the police, and they'll want a word with you.'

Norton pulled a face.

'Will they be long?'

'I shouldn't think so. Feeling all right, Tony?' Asterley went across the hall to the telephone.

'Thanks, yes.'

He felt weaker now that the tension was gone, and his fear subsiding, fear that Sarah would die and that he would never see her again. The realisation of what might have happened made his knees unsteady. He blundered into the drawing-room, and poured himself out a stiff whisky and soda. Asterley came in without speaking, and Norton followed.

Asterley said nothing about the earlier incident. There was little time for saying anything, for Swanley arrived before Tony had finished his drink.

Swanley, in no mood for pleasantries, asked questions in a swift, staccato manner. He listened to the two stories, and almost before Norton had finished speaking, began his questions.

'What time did you leave the club?'

'Nine twenty-five precisely – I'd set my watch by the clock in the Games Room.'

'Who else was there?'

'The usual crowd.'

'I want details, please.'

'Well,' said Norton, 'the Games Room was pretty crowded. The whole cast of the play was on the premises, except Sarah.' He reeled off the names, much as Tony had read them out from the cast list of the script. 'Mrs McNaughton was there, of course, considerably annoyed. Sarah hadn't turned up, so Mrs Mac got Millicent – your daughter – to stand-in. Then Pat was wanted, and couldn't be found. He'd told someone he thought it was a waste of time tonight, and gone off for a drink. We can't get a licence at the club, you might do something about it, Chief!'

Swanley didn't speak.

'Then there was another hunt round for Jim Ellis. He's only got a small, unimportant part. Mrs McNaughton would usually have read it herself, but she went off the deep end. He and Pat often imbibe together, and if one's missing, the other usually is. On the whole, not a successful night.'

'This man you saw on the path – you didn't get a clear view of him?'

'No. He was just a shadow that made a noise, as far as I'm concerned.'

Swanley said: 'I see. Mr Grey, I'd like you to go straight home, I'll come and see you later. Doctor, I'm going to have one of our policewomen in Miss Mellison's room, to take a statement as soon as she is able to make one. Mr Norton,

I'll be grateful if you will be prepared to sign the story you've just told me. It may be needed in evidence. Sergeant – ' he turned to the bulky man who had been taking notes – 'you'll stay here until the policewoman arrives. Then arrange for a special patrol, so that there's no risk of a further attack on Miss Mellison.' The words came out like bullets; Swanley seemed to be fighting back a fierce anger. 'Can you take Mr Grey home, Doctor?'

'Pleased,' murmured Asterley, mildly.

'Thank you. Straight home, mind.' Swanley nodded and went out, letting the door close behind him with a bang.

Norton pushed his hands through his hair.

'Human whirlwind,' he murmured.

They could hear Swanley in the hall, talking to the scared little maid, who answered his questions in a muted voice. For the first time, Tony learned that Sarah's parents were abroad. He heard the maid say:

'Miss Sarah didn't want to go, sir, and stayed behind.'

'I see. When are they due back?'

'The end of next week, sir, but if I send for them – '

'If necessary, I will,' said Swanley. 'I don't want you to tell anyone about this, until I give permission. Is that understood?'

'Oh, I won't say a *word*, sir.'

Asterley was already at the front door. Tony stepped out into the crisp night, and into the big car. Ten minutes later, Tony was sitting in front of the electric fire in the study. He could sit back and relax every throbbing muscle; and that meant that he could wonder what his assailant had expected to get. That packet? If so, Mrs Denton knew something that could help, because presumably she knew what the packet contained.

Swanley arrived just after eleven o'clock. He was curt and abrupt, almost hostile, asking the same questions as at Sarah's house, and receiving the same answers.

'And what else have you to tell me, Mr Grey?'

Tony said: 'Hasn't Asterley told you already?'

'I am not questioning Dr Asterley.'

Tony said: 'Oh, have it your own way. I met Miss Mellison on the common, yesterday afternoon. There didn't seem any point in making her stay there, and so – ' he paused, and then told the story in full detail.

Swanley didn't comment throughout it, nor did he refer to the earlier omissions. When he left, his coldness was as marked as before, but some of the hostility had gone out of it.

The next day was Saturday.

Tony woke up just after seven o'clock, and found that there was only one policeman on duty inside the house. Tony went down to make his own tea; the policeman refused a cup and was more aloof than he had been the day before. Tony shaved and dressed, pondering over a dozen things, most of them leading to Sarah. He wished he had a telephone; at one time he had professed to be glad he wasn't pestered with the ringing, but he needed one now.

He half-expected Asterley to come, but there was no visit; by half past ten, he was sure that he wouldn't see Asterley until later in the day.

He went out, and telephoned Sarah's house. The maid told him that she had slept well, and was much better; and that the policewoman was still on the premises.

The only thing he knew for certain was that he had succeeded in drawing the darkest suspicion of the police upon himself, without doing himself or Sarah any good. The folly of it! He couldn't get the thought of Sarah out of his mind. It was useless to pretend that she didn't matter; she was important. Little he knew about her was in her favour, but she obsessed him.

Why shouldn't he go to see her?

Swanley could hardly be surprised if he did; couldn't read anything sinister into it. He was still free to do what he liked.

He was in that mood at twelve o'clock, when he left the house, but he didn't get beyond the gate. The parcel postman arrived, his little red van squealing to a standstill.

' 'Morning, sir. Mr Grey?'

'Yes.'

'Registered parcel, Mr Grey.'

It was a small package, heavily sealed with brown gummed paper, addressed in block lettering. He signed the yellow receipt slip, and went back into the house. He hadn't been expecting a parcel, had not the faintest idea what this could be. The front door was open, and the youthful policeman was staring at the parcel, eyes loaded with suspicion.

Tony nodded, and passed him, took the parcel into the study, was tempted to close the door sharply, but instead, left it open. The policeman stood at the far side of the hall, watching intently. Tony slit the gummed paper with his penknife; it was a difficult parcel to open. Beneath the outside wrapper was more brown paper, almost as heavily sealed. There was still no indication of the sender. He pulled the second wrapping off, and found a small wooden cigar box – the size for twenty-five cigars. There had been a label on it, but that had been torn off.

The lid was fastened down with small nails; he had to get a screwdriver, to force it up. He was acutely conscious of the watching policeman, and in sudden exasperation stood to one side, so that the man could see exactly what he saw.

There was cotton wool in the box.

'Oh, this is crazy!' Tony said aloud, and glanced round. 'Why stay there? Why not come and see that I don't slip anything up my sleeve.'

'Thank you, sir!' The constable came in promptly.

Tony laughed, as he plucked at the cotton wool. It was pressed down thickly, and he couldn't feel anything wrapped up in it. Was this a hoax? Who would want to make a fool of him? What was usually wrapped in cotton wool? He didn't have to waste time guessing.

He felt something hard, beneath a layer of wool, plucked this layer out carefully, and felt it all over. Inside there was something quite small, about the size of a pea. It took a fantastically long time to get the cotton wool away from it, the stuff was fluffy and obstinate. But suddenly he caught a glint, as of glass.

The policeman said: 'Look!'

Tony didn't speak, but pulled the rest of the cotton wool away. Something sparkled, giving off a dozen different shoots of coloured fire. He knew what it was long before it lay on the palm of his hand, winking and gleaming up at him. A diamond, worth a small fortune.

'Excuse me, sir,' said the policeman, 'but you ought to tell the Superintendent about this, right away.'

In his office at the police station, Swanley took the diamond from Tony, examined it closely, then opened a drawer and rummaged in it, pulling out a watchmaker's glass from the back. He switched on a desk light, fixed the glass to his eye, and held the diamond with a pair of tweezers. He stared at it for a long time, turning it this way and that.

Tony watched with increasing excitement. Swanley shared the doubt which had quickly sprung to Tony's mind; doubt whether this was real or paste. He knew nothing about diamonds, but it was hard to believe that this was imitation, the brightness beneath that strong light made it look like silver fire.

Swanley switched the light off, and turned towards Tony. He looked tired, his eyes were red-rimmed; he was suffering under considerable strain.

Tony said huskily: 'Is it real?'

'Yes, it's real,' Swanley said without hesitation. 'Do you know anything about precious stones, Mr Grey?'

'Nothing at all.'

'Have you ever seen this one before?'

'I have not.'

'Have you any idea who sent it to you?'

'No.'

'H'm,' said Swanley, taking the diamond to the desk and dropping it into the box. 'I've given you plenty of chances to tell me the whole truth, Mr Grey, and I'm not satisfied that you have done so yet. I shall have to ask you to stay here, for the time being.'

CHAPTER 17

The Disheartened Policeman

The words should have come with a sickening shock; they didn't. Tony looked back evenly at Swanley; the man was nearly asleep on his feet.

'Are you charging me with murder?'

'For the time being I shall not charge you, but in your own interests and to facilitate inquiries, I want you to stay here. In the morning – '

'No go,' Tony said. 'Either you arrest me on a charge, or I leave. You may not be very impressed by me – I'm certainly not very impressed by you, or rather, by the way you've handled the case.'

Swanley stared at him out of weary, red-rimmed eyes.

'For instance,' Tony continued, fighting down a small glimmer of compassion, 'after the trouble on the common. your men watched my house. They must have seen Mrs Denton go in, but they didn't prevent the attack on me or on her. I was followed last night, and your people let a man on the tow-path get away with it. Just when they should have been on the job they vanished. Blunders pile up on one another. I made one, you've made several, and I'm not going to be talked into staying here for the night.'

Swanley said heavily: 'I see. Perhaps you won't mind waiting here for a few minutes.' He rang a bell, which was answered immediately. 'Stay here with Mr Grey until I come back, sergeant.'

'Yes, sir.'

Tony walked across to the window, and looked out into

the narrow street as the door closed on Swanley.

Swanley crossed the passage outside his office, tapped on a door opposite, and went in on a clear: 'Come in.' Colonel Wilfred Wilson, the Chief Constable of the County, sat at his desk in a small office. He used it much less than Swanley used his, and the Superintendent had the larger office on his Chief's instructions. Wilson was a slender, upright man, with plentiful grey hair and an air of youthfulness. He looked as fresh as Swanley was tired.

'Come in, Tom. Sit down.' He motioned to a chair.

'Thanks.' Swanley sat down. 'It's time you sent for the Yard, you know.'

'What's worrying you now?'

'My own mood,' said Swanley, and lit a cigarette. 'I've been on the go without a stop since we found the body, and can't stand the strain. No one else here can help much, and if I go on like this, I shall fluff it.'

Wilson smiled.

'That isn't likely. I don't want to send for Scotland Yard until after the inquest, anyhow – surprising facts sometimes crop up at inquests. It's a good testing time. Can't you see that through? There's no reason why you shouldn't have a good eight hours sleep tonight, and in the morning you'll feel a new man.' The Chief Constable's mellow voice was pleasant and unhurried.

'I'd expect you to say that. The truth is, I'm beat,' said Swanley. 'I was sure that Grey knew the Dentons. I don't think so now. He's been covering up for Sarah Mellison, and the Lord knows that's human enough. He's just had a parcel sent him. It contained a single diamond worth a couple of thousand pounds, I'd say. The constable on duty saw him open it – at Grey's own invitation. He seemed completely surprised by it.'

'Diamonds,' Wilson said softly. 'But that's what you're looking for. The Yard warned us that Denton was on the inside of a gang of jewel thieves.'

'I don't know for certain that this one was stolen. The

point is that I tried to scare Grey, told him I wanted him to stay here. He took it up, said he'd stay on a charge, but not without one.' Swanley forced a laugh. 'Then he told me, with a certain amount of detail, what he thinks of my handling of the case. Taken by and large, he's about right.'

'I'd rather like to meet this Grey, he seems full of contradictions,' Wilson said.

'He's certainly no fool. I fastened on him, of course, because he was new to the district. Denton wouldn't have come here unless he'd come to sell some stuff. The packet his wife wanted almost certainly contained diamonds, or stolen jewels. I haven't taxed her with that yet, I'd rather let her wait until the inquest. She's volunteered nothing. I think she might crack, during that. If Grey isn't the prospective buyer, who is? Because as I see it, Denton came down to do a deal, and was killed and robbed by the man with whom he hoped to do it. Or the woman.'

'And I don't see why you need alter your opinion,' said Wilson. 'You may have the wrong man in Grey. But we're not yet sure that Grey is a stranger to the Dentons.'

'It's beginning to look that way. The one certain thing is that Denton was killed with one of the baseball bats from the Theatre Club. Someone from outside might have known they were there, but it isn't really likely. There were no prints on it. The evidence points to someone at the club. Sarah Mellison – ' he shrugged. 'She might murder, but not for money, her parents are too well off. It's possible that Denton was blackmailing her, but I've no evidence. Anyhow, men are involved – the men who attacked Mrs Denton and Grey, and – presumably the same men – who attacked Sarah Mellison and Grey last night. These people want that mysterious packet badly.'

'Looking at it rationally, the murderer and the assailants are probably one and the same,' Wilson said.

'I've tried looking at it rationally,' said Swanley. 'I thought I was on to something last night. Young Pat McNaughton and Jim Ellis weren't at the club when the river attack was made. They could have slipped out and attacked the couple, but they were drinking at a nearby pub. I don't see how I can shake their alibi, and don't see how I can assume that either would deal in precious stones. I've checked on everyone in that theatre cast, and none of them was free on the afternoon of the murder – they couldn't have gone to the common. No one was on the club premises except the caretaker who saw Sarah Mellison, and heard someone else – club members drop in casually, there's no very strict watch kept. That made me more than ever sure that Grey was guilty. The attacks make it seem less likely. There's still a possibility that it was Sarah Mellison, but – ' he shrugged. 'Nothing in the way of evidence. Nothing. And I'm all in.'

'Eight hours sleep, and you'll laugh at yourself,' said Wilson. 'What do you make of this present for Grey?'

'I haven't a notion.'

'Where was the package posted from?'

'London, W.C. We'll never trace anyone through that. There are only Grey's and the postman's fingerprints on the wrapping paper, and I had that checked before I talked to him. I thought he might be pulling a fast one, and the threat of detention would really shake him. Instead, it's shaken me!'

Wilson smiled.

'Let him go with warnings ringing in his ears, and then concentrate on the inquest.'

'I suppose that's the answer,' Swanley said, 'but I'll be happier when the Yard's down here.'

'I'll be happier if we catch the beggar ourselves,' said Wilson. 'How is Sarah Mellison?'

'Almost as well as ever, but still in bed and pretending that she's ill. Asterley's been to see her twice today. She tells exactly the same story as Grey, about last night. I can't shake her. She's admitted that she was on the common, but by itself, that's not sufficient to justify an arrest.'

Wilson said: 'Tom, it's not often you lie to me.'

The words affected Swanley like an electric shock. He sat upright and gripped the arms of his chair. Even the weight of tiredness lifted, and his eyes sparkled.

'What the devil do you mean?'

'You haven't told me why you're so depressed.'

'I've told you – '

'Asterley's a good friend of yours, isn't he?' asked Wilson, quietly. 'And a good friend of mine. You can't understand why he's so interested in Grey, why he brought him and Sarah together, why he left it to them to tell you about the meeting on the common. Isn't this true, Tom? Asterley's under your skin. You can't face up to the possibility that a friend is involved. You're not even sure that you can trust your own judgement, because of him. Isn't that true?'

Swanley didn't answer.

Wilson said: 'You may be right and you may be wise. But I still say, get the inquest prepared, have a good sleep, and then you'll see things more clearly. It's preposterous to think that Rick Asterley is involved, and you know it.'

Swanley said, and his voice was searching for enlightenment: 'But is it only preposterous because we're his close friends?'

As Tony walked from the police station, he carried a mental picture of Swanley's face and red-rimmed eyes. He had the impression that Swanley had looked worse, when he had returned to the room, than when he had left it. Little had been said. Just a brusque: 'You can go, Mr Grey, but I must ask you to stay in Wallingham.' To which Tony had replied: 'Until this case is over, nothing will make me leave.' The sergeant had escorted him downstairs, and now he was walking briskly towards the High Street. He was hungry and, in a way, elated. If Swanley had anything on him, he would still be at the police station. The police were guessing.

He caught sight of Mrs McNaughton on the other side of the road, then he saw the slim figure of Anne Denton. Both women glanced across and saw him.

Mrs McNaughton waved, her voice called imperiously: 'Young man!'

She was impossible.

Heads turned to see who it was who had attracted her attention.

Mrs McNaughton bellowed again. Fuming under his breath, his happier mood quite shattered, Tony went across.

'There you are!' boomed Mrs McNaughton. She took Anne Denton's arm, in a possessive grasp. 'Why haven't you been to see this young lady? She's been expecting to hear from you.'

'Mrs McNaughton, please!'

'Oh, you didn't say so, but I can tell,' said the older woman, and her raddled face was twisted in a smile that was intended to be knowing. 'You ought to have come, Tony, it's too bad of you to stay away. We're just going to have luncheon, will you join us?'

'No! I – I'm awfully sorry, I've an appointment I can't miss.' She actually made him stammer. 'It's frightfully good of you, but –'

'I don't know that I believe you,' said Mrs McNaughton. 'Do you, Anne?'

After that first sharp protest, Anne Denton seemed to have resigned herself to the inevitable. There was a smile in her eyes; they were good eyes, and much calmer than when he had seen her before. With a sense of shock, he realised that she looked rested, as if the stay with the theatrical Mrs McNaughton had done her good.

'Of course I believe him.'

Mrs McNaughton waved this betrayal magnanimously away.

'But you're to come tomorrow evening, I won't take no for an answer. Off with you!'

Tightening her grip on Anne's arm she marched her towards the restaurant in which Tony himself had intended to have lunch. He turned in the opposite direction, glumly reviewing the Rose and Crown in his mind's eye. He would probably enjoy the atmosphere of the pub far more, he told himself, and there would certainly be less likelihood of encountering prying eyes.

As he marched along, Pat McNaughton roared past him in his red two-seater, a fluffy-haired girl sitting by his side. Both the McNaughtons had a love of display in common, he thought sourly, and the spectacular.

The dining-room of the Rose and Crown was on the first floor. Following the waitress, he saw with relief that no one appeared to be interested in him. He could think at leisure about his minor triumph over Swanley; about Sarah; about Anne Denton.

He was surprised at the change in her. He had thought that she would take weeks to recover from the shock, but laughter not far removed from gaiety had been in her eyes when she had smiled at him.

Hadn't she been as distressed as she'd made out?

It might be a good idea to see her before tomorrow evening, after all. He had become deeply involved in this affair, whether he wanted to be or not, perhaps it would be less depressing if he took a more active part, rather than wait docilely for the next assault. He could start his investigations with Anne.

Or with Sarah.

Looking up, he saw Pat McNaughton enter the room, his eyes looking round searchingly, finally coming to rest at his own table. McNaughton had inherited little from his mother but her vitality and bombastic love of display. He was tall, fair-haired and slender, a man possessed of a gallivanting recklessness which appealed to most women and many men. Junior partner in a small firm of estate agents, he spent most of his time running round the countryside, looking at available properties. He was a man whom Tony liked, with reservations; it was impossible not to be charmed by his open delight in the good things of life, his complete indifference to what others thought of him.

'Hallo, Grey.' He pulled up a chair and sat down. 'I've been looking for you everywhere. Great luck running you to earth. Finished?'

'Yes.'

'Good. Sarah wants to see you. She's in a terrific flap about something. I told her I'd take you along, even if I had to shanghai you.' He laughed, ignoring, though probably enjoying, the gaze of everyone in the room. 'Ready?'

CHAPTER 18

Fear

Tony had not seen the residential district near the river by daylight. It had an atmosphere of wealth and aloofness. The houses stood back in their own grounds, their expensive garages decently screened by wistaria. Wherever one looked, neat lawns and herbaceous borders met the eye.

The red sports car snorted up to one of the most perfect of its type, and jolted to a standstill.

'As instructed,' said McNaughton, grinning. 'Want me to come in and hold your hand?'

'Want me to guess whether the offer is wholly disinterested?'

'There's more in you than I realised,' declared McNaughton. 'For once, my old lady was right!'

'Thanks for the lift.'

Tony opened the gate and looked at the house, contrasting it rather grimly with his own. A sloping lawn, on which no daisy would have dared to show its head, was broken by a pool, where darting goldfish caught the sun. It was a garden in which no tree straggled, no flower bloomed unstaked, unlabelled.

He caught a glimpse of Sarah, passing a window. She moved quickly out of sight, but he had had time to see the pallor of her face and to judge by it that she was really frightened. He quickened his pace. McNaughton's car roared away into the distance, and the sound had faded by the time Tony reached the front door. He was admitted by the young maid he had seen before, shown into the room in which he had been the previous night. Sarah was standing there. She looked nervous, and ill at ease. As the door closed, she came forward quickly, and took his hands.

'Tony, I'm so scared.'

'There probably isn't any need to be.' Was this just fear, because of what had happened the previous night? Did she lack even physical courage? 'What's worrying you?'

'I – I've had an anonymous letter.'

'Burn it, and forget about it,' he said promptly.

'It's not as simple as that.' She withdrew her hands and went to the window, stood with her back to him, looking out. 'I had to see you. You probably hate the sight of me, after last night. But I'll never be able to thank you for what you did. It was – '

'Forget it!' His tone was rough.

'I shan't do that,' she said, more calmly, and turned her head to look at him. 'No, I'll never do that. Tony, do you know why they pushed me in?'

'It was only one man, and I think he pushed us in by accident.'

'No,' said Sarah. 'No, that isn't true.' Dramatically she held out a letter which had been tucked in the front of her dress. 'Look!'

The envelope was white, and of cheap quality. He opened it slowly, conscious of Sarah's increasing tension. He read:

> It's no use holding out on us, you and your clever friend Grey will suffer if you don't cough up. We know enough to get *you* a life sentence, sweetie. Tell Grey we want that packet, and he's to be ready to hand it over.

Tony read it twice before he looked up. Sarah's eyes were too bright, too indicative of fear.

'Do you see what it means?' She clenched her hands. 'I ought to burn it and laugh at it, but I can't. It came just before lunch. I tried to pretend it didn't matter, but it wasn't a bit of use. I found myself shivering one moment, too hot to breathe the next. I suppose I haven't recovered from the shock of last night. Tony, I didn't kill Denton.'

He found himself saying: 'Of course you didn't.'

'I don't think you really believe that,' said Sarah. 'I don't think anyone does. Swanley was here again, this morning. He didn't accuse me, but – '

'He was trying to shake you. He did the same to me. I shouldn't worry about Swanley. There's nothing he can prove, it would be different if you were a friend of Denton or even if you knew him.' He picked up a cigarette box and held it out to her. 'Have a cigarette, and – '

'But I did know Ray Denton,' Sarah said.

He was so startled that he nearly dropped the box. He put it down quickly, looking at her all the time. She was shivering.

'I've known him for years,' she said. 'I was going to meet him, on the common.'

Still Tony didn't speak.

'We met in France. I rather liked him. I was with two girl friends, and as we hadn't any money, he cashed cheques for us. It seemed clever to get French money we weren't supposed to have. We had a wild time, he was with us most of the holiday.' She was talking mechanically, now, anxious to get it said. 'Soon afterwards, there was a lot of trouble over English people having cheques cashed in France, and quite a number of prosecutions. I was nervous, and – he wrote and asked me to see him in London about it.'

She paused.

'Yes,' said Tony, and his mouth was dry.

'I went, of course. He seemed terribly worried, said that he'd managed to keep clear of trouble, but he'd had to bribe a lot of people to keep their mouths shut. He asked me to help him with money, and wanted a hundred pounds. I didn't hesitate, but gave him a cheque, on my London bank. We went and cashed it together. I didn't hear anything more for some months, and then there was another big prosecution. He wrote and said exactly the same thing. I gave him fifty pounds, that time. Then – two months ago – he came to see me here. My mother and father were out, I was alone with Hetty, the maid. That was the first time I realised that he was blackmailing me. We had a row, and I gave him nothing. After that, he worried me by letter and by telephone, and I sent him another fifty pounds.'

Tony said: 'The swine,' very softly.

'I heard from him the day before he was killed. He said he had to see me again, and I arranged to meet him on the common. You know what happened. I didn't kill him, Tony, but who'll believe me if all this comes out?'

Tony went to her, and slipped his arm round her shoulders. She was trembling. He led her to a couch, and they sat down. She leaned against him, then gave a convulsive sob, and buried her face against his shoulder; as it had happened before.

'Now tell me I'm a coward, and a fool,' she said, huskily. 'I am, I know it. That letter finished me. I had to talk to someone, and you saved my life, which makes you, in a way, responsible for me, doesn't it? What shall I do, Tony? I can't just sit back and wait for things to happen! As this man's written me a letter, he might write to someone else; perhaps to the police. If I lie to them –'

'No more lies,' Tony said.

'But supposing –'

'The only thing that will get us through is the truth. When we know who killed Denton, we'll be safe ourselves. Don't wait for the police to get anonymous letters, tell them yourself.'

She pulled away from him, lighting a cigarette, drawing on it fiercely.

'They already know how desperately anxious I was that they shouldn't discover I was on the common. Won't they add two and two together, and assume that I did it?'

'They might – but they'll need a lot of evidence. This may make you Suspect Number 1, but it isn't evidence they are likely to take to court. They'll want something much stronger. They might –' he leaned back, and his hands were tightly clenched. 'They might detain you. I don't know. I do know that you'll be crazy to tell them anything but the truth.'

Sarah stubbed out the cigarette, and immediately groped for another.

'I suppose you're right,' she said, and looked at the telephone. 'I suppose Swanley will be in. I don't like him, but at least he's – fair. Tony, will you telephone – '

She broke off, and glanced out of the window. Tony had been so intent on her, that he had heard and noticed nothing. Now he saw a car draw up; a large black Austin. Even before Swanley got out, he knew that it was the detective's car. Swanley and two others came up the drive, walking abreast; large, powerful men, purposeful in manner.

Sarah said: 'Tony!'

He jumped up and gripped her shoulders, shaking her slightly.

'Sarah, listen to me! You've got to get a grip on yourself. You've got to behave as if you were innocent, if you go on like this, they might well jump to the wrong conclusions. This may be just another inquiry, but you can tell Swanley everything. I'll stay – he can't make me leave. Face it out, Sarah. Face it, understand?' He gave her another little shake.

There was a tap at the door, and the maid said nervously:

'Please, Miss Sarah, there's the Superintendent, he wants to see you again.'

Sarah didn't speak.

'Please, Miss Sarah – '

Tony said roughly: 'Ask him to come in!' He put his mouth close to Sarah's ear, and whispered: 'It's up to you. You can carry this off, if you want to. Face up to it.'

She broke away from him, turned to look in the mirror over the fireplace, went to the table and took a powder compact from her handbag. She was powdering her nose when Swanley came in, alone. He seemed surprised to see Tony; unpleasantly? He looked even more tired than before lunch, but his voice was firm.

'Good afternoon, Miss Mellison.' He ignored Tony. 'I'm

sorry to have to worry you again, but I would like your permission to search the house.'

Sarah said: '*Search?*' She passed the puff over her cheeks. Nothing could hide the fact that she had been crying or that she was on edge, but her voice was stronger, and she was making a big effort to keep her self control. 'Why on earth do you want to search?'

'It is necessary,' Swanley said formally.

Sarah looked at Tony, as if for help. He didn't speak, could do nothing more to help.

'Very well, but before you start, there is something I would like to say to you.' Her voice was high and strained. 'Is that shorthand writer of yours with you? So much easier for him to start at the beginning, than wait until the middle and ask me to repeat the whole thing over again.'

Swanley said: 'Yes, he's here. Bennett!' The big man who looked so absurd with the little notebook, stepped in quickly. 'Do I understand that you wish to volunteer a statement about the death of Mr Raymond Denton, Miss Mellison?'

'Oh, no. But about my association with him. I know nothing about his death – you'll write that down, Mr Bennett, won't you?' Her voice was still high, and a little unnatural, but compared with her behaviour a few minutes before, she was magnificent. 'I'm afraid it's a melancholy story, Mr Swanley, and it started some time ago, when I was on holiday in France . . .'

It was over. The notebook was shut, and tucked away.

Sarah stood looking out of the window. Bennett was by the door. Tony, feeling as if he were suspended in mid-air, stood by the fireplace, smoking a cigarette. The movements of the other two men upstairs could be heard faintly.

It was twenty minutes since Sarah had finished the statement; Swanley had thanked her, formally, and asked Bennett to wait with them. He had not otherwise acknowledged Tony's presence.

The sounds became louder; Swanley was coming downstairs. Sarah didn't look at the door, but Tony saw the way in which her shoulders moved, as if she were squaring them to face the inevitable.

Swanley came in. He held something clenched tightly in his hand. He still looked tired, but there was a new factor – excitement, almost a look of triumph. He glanced at Tony, then shrugged as if Tony didn't matter, went to Sarah and stood just behind her.

'Miss Mellison, will you look at these, please?'

She turned, slowly. Swanley was quite close to her, watching her intently. He stretched out his hand, and the sunlight flashed on to jewels which lay on the palm.

Sarah's start was not violent – it could have been caused by surprise, even dismay. She looked frankly into Swanley's face.

'Are these yours?' Swanley asked.

'Why, yes.'

'All of them?'

'All four,' she said.

'I see,' said Swanley, and closed his fingers over the jewels. 'I must ask you to come with me, Miss Mellison. It is my duty to charge you with being in possession of precious stones, knowing them to have been stolen, and to warn you that anything you say may be used in evidence.'

CHAPTER 19

Inquest Verdict

Sarah stared at Swanley with surprise; astonishment. What he said was obviously entirely different to what she had expected him to say. Swanley stood like a statue, and Bennett and the other man moved forward from the doorway, as if they expected her to resist. Bennett took up a position only a foot away from Tony, and watched him, not the girl.

Sarah said: 'But that's absurd! They're mine.'

'They are stolen jewels, Miss Mellison, in your possession.'

'But they were given to me by –'

'Hold it!' Tony snapped the words, and moved forward, brushing Bennett aside. 'Don't say anything, Sarah, except that you didn't know they were stolen. Who is your family's solicitor?'

'But, Tony –'

'Mr Grey, I must ask you to leave this room,' said Swanley, in a harsh voice. 'Sergeant –'

'I've told you what I think about the way you've handled this case,' Tony said sharply. 'Trying to trick Miss Mellison into making a statement against her own interests gives you another black mark.'

'Mr Grey!' thundered Swanley, and Bennett's large hand fell upon Tony's arm.

Tony didn't try to pull himself free.

'You can't have it both ways, Swanley. You wanted me here to see whether I showed any evidence of guilt – and I'm here. Sarah, you have every right to demand to see a solicitor, and he would advise you not to say a word until you've discussed this with him thoroughly. You can't tell what fantastic twist Swanley will put on anything you say. Just sit tight.'

She looked at him, smiling, with more than a hint of courage in her eyes; it was surprising, coming just then, and yet he was not really surprised. She had touched the depth of fear and depression, and her spirit was rising again.

'All right, Tony. Thanks. See Mr Wray for me, will you – Nathaniel Wray, of Wray and Robertson, in the High Street.'

'I will!'

'Do you mind if I get some clothes, Mr Swanley?' Sarah asked, and her tone was light again. It was almost as if she were relieved, now that the worst had happened; and possibly because the charge was one which, to her, made nonsense.

'Where did you get those jewels?'

'I'd like to consult Mr Wray,' Sarah said.

'Miss Mellison, I want to know – '

'Later, perhaps. May I get my clothes?'

'Your maid can fetch what you require,' Swanley said, choking. 'Sergeant, take Miss Mellison into the hall, please.'

He waited until they had gone, and he was alone in the room with Tony. He looked aggressive and angry, but kept his voice low.

'Why did you come here, Mr Grey?'

'Miss Mellison asked me to come.'

'Why?'

'She wanted my advice. She told me what she has told you, and I advised her to tell you at the first opportunity.'

'Did you know anything about it before?'

'No. In spite of this.'

He showed Swanley the letter. Swanley read it very carefully, folded it neatly into his pocket, but was not to be deflected from his main interest.

'Have you ever seen these before?' He held the jewels out, starkly displayed on his large, pink palm.

'I may have done. Miss Mellison may have worn them

when we met,' Tony said. 'I've never handled them, if that's what you mean. Why don't you stop guessing, Superintendent?'

'We do not work by guessing,' Swanley said, 'and we do not act until we have certain knowledge. I shall want to see you again, Mr Grey. Be sure that you don't leave Wallingham without informing us where you are going.'

The last Tony saw of Sarah, that day, was as she climbed into Swanley's car. Her head was held high, she showed the grace which had captivated him from the beginning. She smiled at him, and then the door closed, and hid her from sight.

He walked back to Wallingham.

Mr Nathaniel Wray, senior partner in the largest firm of solicitors in Wallingham, did not impress Tony favourably. He was elderly, fussy and formal, more shocked and worried that such a misfortune could overtake one of his clients, rather than because it had happened to Sarah, as a person. He promised to visit the police station at once. But he showed no sign of being ready to leave the office when Tony left.

Now that there was nothing else to do, Tony walked aimlessly along the crowded High Street. Saturday afternoons were busier than most. In the broad stretch of the market, the stalls clustered like dark beehives. Above the voices of bellowing salesmen rose the smell of vegetables, fruit, meat and fish. The shops were equally crowded, but few people took any notice of Tony. Outwardly untroubled, he strolled towards Asterley's house. The Sunbeam Talbot stood outside the front entrance. He turned in at the gates, catching a glimpse of Asterley through the drawing-room window.

The maid answered the door.

'Are Dr and Mrs Asterley alone?' asked Tony.

'Please to come in. I am to ask you, if you call,' emphatically pronounced the maid, in her stilted English.

So Asterley had half-expected him.

The maid opened the door, as Asterley was saying:

'It doesn't make any difference, dear, whether I'm away for three weeks or four. I'd rather make it four, we'll probably get a better *locum* for the full month than for part of one. Ginger will probably – ' he broke off. 'Yes, Anna, who is it?'

'Please, Mr Grey.'

'Tony!' There was no questioning the note of welcome, and Asterley came forward as the maid moved back. 'Just in time for a cup of tea!' He drew Tony in. 'Dora, our luck's in, we have the most celebrated man in Wallingham calling on us.'

Dora Asterley smiled a welcome.

'I hope you won't be disturbed this time, Mr Grey. Rick, push up a chair.'

The friendliness was as marked as ever, but as Mrs Asterley poured tea, Asterley frowned into Tony's face, as if he knew already that there was news of importance.

'More anxiety, Tony?'

'Yes. Sarah's really in a mess this time.'

A thin clatter, as if a cup or saucer had been put down too hastily, came from Mrs Asterley. It was the first time Tony had seen her startled enough to reveal it.

'Sarah, eh?' Asterley was grave. 'I saw her this morning. She seemed fairly sensible then, and sorry she made a fool of herself the other night. Is it serious?'

'Very,' said Tony, and told them.

Asterley was silent for several minutes afterwards, and his wife, already pale, seemed to lose what colour she had. Tony's tea was poured out, but she forgot to hand it to him. It was as if they'd just had broken to them news of a gravely personal nature.

Asterley looked broodingly into the fire.

'Well, it certainly doesn't sound too good. Sarah isn't the reckless, sophisticated wench she likes to pretend, and she'll take this hard. It's a pity her parents are away, the mother isn't much help, but her father is all right. Nat Wray –

well, he's a good lawyer, but this isn't quite his cup of tea. Don't see how we can alter that, though. Talking of tea – ' he forced a laugh. 'Where's Tony's, darling?'

'Oh, I'm so sorry. No, it'll be cold, I'll pour you out another. Rick, I've never had such a shock.'

'She was behaving pretty oddly,' said Asterley, frowning. 'This explains it, of course, but Sarah couldn't have killed him. It's unthinkable!' But the way he spoke meant that he was beginning to wonder. 'How did she take it, Tony?'

'Pretty well, but screwed up to a pitch that can't last.'

'Anyhow, it was a good thing you were there. She is too volatile, too easily stung to be safe near a policeman's notebook without a cautioning hand. At least it takes some of the weight off you, Tony.'

'Does it?'

'One kind of weight, anyhow.' Asterley looked at him thoughtfully. 'Hum. Well, we'll have to see what we can do. I'll have a word with Wray, although Swanley will probably think I shouldn't. He takes a dim view of some of my activities already, I can sense that.' He laughed, but there was no amusement in it. 'Is there anything you would particularly like me to do?'

'Yes. Find out how Mrs McNaughton has managed to cheer Mrs Denton up so much,' Tony said.

'Oh, that! Mrs McNaughton is a tonic in herself – it's impossible for anyone to brood when they're with her. That's no mystery. Anything else?'

'I don't think so,' said Tony. 'Do you know when the inquest is to be held?'

'Hasn't Swanley told you? Monday morning. Ten o'clock.'

'Then we've a weekend to work in,' Tony said.

In fact, it was an infuriating weekend; there was so much he wanted to do, so little he could. He was no longer followed, and there were no more incidents. The statement that Sarah was under arrest had spread by the evening. He heard her name on a dozen different lips; the town was agog. Pat McNaughton, Ellis, Norton and several other members of the club called to see him, vaguely offering goodwill and help. Most of them appeared to be shocked. Nothing could shock McNaughton, but he was grim about the prospects.

Tony went to the McNaughtons' house early on the Sunday evening. It was a big, rambling place, not far from his own. He hoped to see Anne Denton, but she didn't appear, pleading a headache. It did not match up with the glimpse he'd had of her in the High Street the day before. There were other guests, but they were older than he, and there were few club members. Mrs McNaughton, richly upholstered in peacock blue, practically ignored him. The visit was a failure, only emphasising that he felt flat and helpless, unable to judge his own emotions dispassionately. It was as if part of him was locked up in that dingy building with Sarah.

He woke early on Monday morning, tossed and turned, and was up soon after half-past six; hours dragging with leaden feet until ten o'clock.

The courtroom was crowded. The jury appeared to be composed entirely of men, but for one tight-lipped woman who glared at him throughout. He hoped it was nervousness, or short-sight, but feared malevolence. The Coroner had at least one good point; he didn't waste time. Witness after witness was called and banished, some of them appearing to have little to do with the case.

Anne Denton gave formal identification of her husband's body. Dressed in black, she looked small and subdued; and there was now no sign of Mrs McNaughton's tonic effect.

A nervous and poorly dressed man, Ray Denton's brother, said that he hadn't been told about the marriage, but knew that Ray had 'business' in Wallingham, and had once heard him mention a woman's name: 'Sarah'.

That brought a rustle of excitement. The Coroner called for silence, but the tension quickened. It increased when Sarah was called. The Coroner asked his questions in flat, unemotional tones which seemed to make the atmosphere even more electric. Sarah was composed; her eyes looked heavy, but her beauty threw everything else into shadowed gloom. Nathaniel Wray stood by her side, like a well-groomed blackbird, until she went into the witness box.

Then the questions came; swift, damning.

'You knew the deceased?'

'Yes.'

'You had paid him money from time to time, in return for his discretion where an offence which you had committed was concerned?'

'Yes.'

'You had an assignation with him on Hoodle Common on the afternoon of his death?'

'Yes.' The single word was clear, and the silence so tense that a whisper could have been heard.

'Had you reason to believe that he would make further demands?'

'Yes.'

It went on and on. Nathaniel Wray was worse than useless, bobbed up now and again, to make a weak protest, and bobbed down again. The Coroner started to talk about the baseball bats.

'You know, I believe, that there were four of these bats at the Theatre Club?'

'Yes.'

'In your statement, you have said that you took part, one evening, in using them as Indian clubs.'

'Yes.'

'But my client has made it *quite* clear that she did not take one from the club-room – the stage,' piped Nathaniel Wray.

'Evidence of that may be taken in another court, but not this one,' said the Coroner. 'Yes. You may stand down, Miss Mellison – unless you have questions to ask the witness, Mr Wray?'

'No, at this stage, no,' said Nathaniel. 'No!'

In the court, near the back, Mrs McNaughton was heard to utter a profound 'Fool!' No one laughed, no one seemed to take any notice – except the Coroner, who stared icily towards the spot from which the interruption had come, but omitted to call for silence.

'Very well,' he said. 'Ladies and gentlemen of the jury, you have heard the evidence, and as you know it is your duty to say how, in your opinion, the deceased met his death. In view of the medical evidence, most admirably given, if I may say so, there can hardly be two opinions. It is not, you understand, any part of your duty to go beyond making a simple statement as to whether you consider the deceased died by accident, by his own hand, or by the hand of another. You may, however, add any rider which, after full consideration, you may feel is indicated by the evidence you have heard. Do you wish to retire to consider your verdict?'

There was whispering among the jury; and a burly man rather like Bennett, the foreman, stood up.

'We do not wish to retire, your honour.'

'Very well. What is your verdict?'

The hush was agonising. Tony could see no one else but Sarah; Sarah's great grey-green eyes, beautiful, curiously calm. Sarah, standing by Nathaniel Wray's side, much more relaxed than anyone could have expected.

'We find, your honour, that the deceased was murdered and wish to add a rider, your honour.'

'What is that rider?'

'That the deceased was killed by Miss Sarah Mellison.'

There was a tense silence which seemed to last for minutes; and then a woman shouted at the back of the court, and hubbub broke loose.

CHAPTER 20

Promise

The Coroner's furious rapping on the table in front of him failed to silence the crowd. Reporters were already struggling in a wild mêlée to get out of the courtroom.

Tony stood up and moved across the seething court, climbed over the rails which separated the witnesses from the rest of the room, ignored Sergeant Bennett's wave of protest, and reached Sarah.

Asterley was saying: 'It's absurd, Sarah, and we'll soon have everything put right.'

'Thank you,' Sarah said mechanically.

'Miss Mellison – ' Swanley began.

Tony pushed past him. At closer quarters, he could see that Sarah's calm was cracking. All her colour had gone, and her eyes were enormous.

He gripped her hands, as she had often gripped his.

'Sarah, listen. I'll spend every minute I can, every penny I have, proving what fools they've made of themselves. Understand?' His voice was unsteady.

She looked at him.

'Thank you – Tony.'

He could only just hear the words.

'And listen. I love you.' The words were flung out. 'I love you.'

Sarah gasped: 'Don't!' and closed her eyes.

Swanley, pushing past him, took her arm and, with Wray on the other side, led her out of the courtroom.

Asterley said lightly: 'So, Sir Galahad rides again.'

*

Furious and unhappy, Tony made his way to Wray's office, a few hours later. The little solicitor bowed patiently beneath the storm.

'Yes, Mr Grey, there is a great deal in what you say, but Miss Mellison has not been helpful. She refuses to tell me who gave her those jewels. It's a great pity – a great pity.'

'Why won't she say?'

'I wish I knew. However, I have telephoned her father in Paris. He may have more influence, but she is a headstrong young woman. Most.'

They had to leave it at that.

Crowds surged about the newsvendors when the early editions of the London evening newspapers reached Wallingham. Tony, coming out of Wray's office, didn't join the crowd, didn't want to see a newspaper. Sarah made a complicated matter more confused.

He was near the bridge when he heard a man call out:

'Tony – just a minute.'

He turned round, to see Norton on his bicycle, with a newspaper sticking out of his pocket.

'Seen this?' Norton asked, as he drew up and steadied himself with a foot against the kerb.

'No.'

Norton handed him the folded paper. On the front page was a large picture of himself coming out of the court; and above it, three words: I LOVE YOU. Beneath was a caption: 'Anthony Grey, the writer, who forced his way through the police cordon to tell Miss Sarah Mellison that he loved her and would spend every penny he possessed to fight for her freedom.'

Norton was smiling crookedly.

'No one who lived long in Wallingham would have said that, Tony. We're a timid lot – especially those who've always professed to worship her. If I can help at any time, call on me.'

'Thanks.' Tony handed back the paper.

'Keep it,' said Norton, and pushed away from the kerb and cycled on.

There were five newspapermen outside the house, including the tall man who had been there before, and two others who had helped to drink his beer.

'Sorry,' he said. 'No comment.'

'Any fresh line, Grey?' one asked.

'What's this about stolen jewels?'

'Did you know that Denton was a dealer in jewels – contact man for several gangs of jewel thieves?'

'Let's assume that I didn't know,' Tony said.

'Now, listen.' This was the tall man. 'We want to help. This is a big case, we'll all run it as hard as we can – and we may know a thing or two you don't. If you're serious in wanting to clear the lady's name, you'll have to try everything.'

Tony said: 'Oh, all right. Here's a statement. I do not believe that Miss Mellison is guilty, I am quite sure that someone else was hiding on the common, equally sure that we'll find them.'

'Any comment on the police?' asked the tall reporter.

Tony forced a grin. 'Nothing suitable for publication! Personally, I'd be happier if Scotland Yard were handling the case, but that's neither here nor there.'

'A nice quote,' the friendly reporter said, 'damning without being openly insulting. If anything crops up, here's my card – I'm staying at the Rose & Crown.'

'Thanks,' said Tony.

He turned and went in, and no one tried to detain him. The house seemed empty and desolate, yet was exactly the same as it had always been, except that no policeman was there. He went moodily through into the kitchen.

He'd missed his lunch, and it was now past tea time, but he didn't feel like eating, and certainly wasn't going out for a meal. He felt that he didn't want to talk to Asterley or anyone, only to get his own thoughts in order. He spread the newspaper out and stared at the picture. As a photograph, it was a good one. He read the three words: I LOVE YOU. His lips twisted wryly as he said aloud:

'Do I?'

In the highly emotional frame of mind at the courtroom, he'd meant it. Was it true? He wasn't sure, and if it were true, surely he couldn't be in any doubt. He leaned back against the dresser, frowning. He'd talked a lot of nonsense. There was nothing he could really do. Sarah wouldn't need money; it had just been hot air.

He began to cut some bread, and when taking the newspaper off the table, uncovered the reporter's card. There was a message scribbled over the printed words, and he read:

'I'm coming round tonight, late. News of importance.'

Tony read the name printed on the right hand corner: *Arthur Jameson*. Was it true, or just a reporter's trick to get more information? He felt cheered up, for the first time since the inquest verdict.

There was a ring at the front door bell.

He glanced along the passage leading to the front door. It might be another reporter, or Asterley – or someone who just wanted to talk. He was 'news' and would continue to be news for some time. He'd be the butt of all the cranks and fanatics in Wallingham. If only he could get out of the place!

He laughed, abruptly. The bell rang again.

He went along to the front door, gripped the handle tightly, ready to slam it in the caller's face, if needs be.

The light shone on Anne Denton.

If she had been accused of the murder, she couldn't have looked worse. She was tidy enough, and made up, but there were dark shadows under her eyes. He couldn't understand what had made her so cheerful for those few hours; and couldn't understand why she had come now, after refusing to see him at Mrs McNaughton's.

He led her into the study.

'Satisfied?' he growled; and immediately wished that he hadn't spoken so roughly. 'Can I offer you a drink?'

'No, thank you.' She sat down easily, without waiting to

be asked. 'No, I'm not satisfied,' she said slowly. 'I've just come from the police station.'

'Haven't they finished with you, yet?'

'Sometimes I think they never will. Mr Grey, I don't want vengeance, and God knows I don't want to see the wrong person convicted for Ray's death. I've told the police everything I can, at the very least I ought to tell you. Some of it might help – I can't see how, but it might.'

He stood by the fireplace, with his back to it, listening.

'I'm not just trying to get sympathy,' Anne went on. 'I'm simply telling you the truth. I met and fell in love with Ray, and we were married after we'd known each other for three months. I knew nothing about him. We met at lunch one day – I'd just got my job, and had lunch in Wallingham. He was there, we shared a table for two, and – well, it was like a fire, nothing could stop it. I only knew what he cared to tell me about himself, and that was very little. I know now that he was a thief and a criminal, that he dealt in stolen jewels, and wasn't above blackmail.'

Tony looked away from her.

'I didn't even suspect the truth, until two days ago,' she went on stonily. 'It was just after we met in the High Street. Mrs McNaughton had been very helpful, and I was beginning to feel better. Then I saw the police, and discovered that Ray had been dealing in these stolen gems. I discovered something else, too. You – you remember those photographs?'

'Of course.' He'd wasted hours, wondering what significance they could have.

'Apparently the girls were friends of his, who sold some of the jewels for him. Members of the gang. That's what I understood, from Swanley – he didn't say so, but made it pretty clear. And – ' she hesitated, breathing more quickly. 'At least one of them thought she was married to him. Perhaps the others did. The only thing certain is that I was *not* his wife.'

Tony said: 'Oh, my dear!' He moved forward, but something in her manner made him draw back. Compassion for her drove everything else out of his mind.

'This isn't proved yet, but it's true. You remember I asked you if you had that packet. It contained several diamond rings. I – I'd never had an engagement ring. Ray told me he'd several on approval, we were to choose the one that afternoon. He telephoned me, a couple of hours before, and talked about the packet – and it must have contained stolen rings. Then the dreadful thing happened, I hardly knew what I was doing, and – I just couldn't talk about the rings or anything. Can you understand that?'

'Yes, I can see,' said Tony. 'I can understand a great deal I couldn't before.' Silently, he added: 'If all this is true.' Looking at her, it was almost impossible to believe that she was lying. She seemed to have shrunk, and to be much older; worry seemed to have that effect on women.

'That's everything,' she said. 'I felt that you ought to know. I don't know whether Swanley still suspects you. I can't see why he should. Of course – ' She stood up, and toyed with her handbag. 'It's easy to see why we were attacked – someone thinks you have those jewels, because – someone took them away from Ray. And as we were both attacked by Ray's friends, I suppose they didn't have them. And he did come down here to meet Sarah Mellison. Everything seems to point to her.'

Tony nodded.

The attacks could be explained by that. But would anyone go to such lengths for a few jewels?

Anne Denton said sharply: 'What's the matter? Why are you looking like that?'

'Er – sorry. Just an idea.'

It was the obvious idea, but it hadn't struck so forcibly before. The value of that packet must be enormous, for men to take such risks to get it. And every attack they made would suggest to Swanley that they knew Tony had the packet.

'I shall stay at Hoodle for a little while,' Anne Denton said. 'If I can help, just let me know.'

She offered her hand, now much more composed. With

Sarah, quick changes of mood were to be expected. They weren't with this girl. She might have told the whole truth, she might have come simply to make him think that there was nothing else she could tell him.

'Good luck,' he said, as he took her to the door.

'Thanks.'

She nodded, and turned away, walking quickly towards the street. Watching her, he saw that she turned left, away from the main road, and that puzzled him. To get to the bus for Hoodle, she ought to have turned right.

He went after her, keeping to the grass so as to muffle the sound of his footsteps. Hers sounded clearly for a few seconds, and then stopped. When he reached the street, she was nowhere in sight. She hadn't crossed the road; the sudden silence in itself proved that.

He walked on, slowly – and then heard the engine of a car start up. It was parked in the drive of a house several doors along; a house with a 'For Sale' board up. Then the car nosed its way slowly out of the open gates.

It was Pat McNaughton's red two-seater.

CHAPTER 21

New Suspect?

The car turned left, before swinging round towards the river. The hood was up, and it was unlikely that anyone would be able to recognise Pat McNaughton's companion.

Was there anything really odd about this? Anne *was* staying with his mother.

But there was no reason why the car should be parked so furtively off the road. Anne had said that she had come straight from the police, yet McNaughton had been waiting for her. He could have brought her away from Swanley, but why had he decided to let her pay this call alone? He wasn't a man who cared about other people's opinion; wasn't one to behave furtively.

What did he know about Pat McNaughton?

His general popularity, his heartiness, his devil-may-care attitude to life, his estate business, which rested lightly on his shoulders, and – inevitable with a man of that kind – his reputation as being a bit of a roué. It was impossible to believe that he would be furtive for the sake of it. The only conclusion was, then, that he hadn't wanted Tony to know he was waiting for Anne. For a man who normally enjoyed so keenly seeing, and being seen, the car hood wouldn't have been up unless they were anxious to make sure Anne wasn't recognised.

McNaughton had been in a pub near the tow-path on the night of the attack; had plenty of opportunity to be at the common and to meet Ray Denton. There was the old story, too, that McNaughton had bitterly resented it when Sarah had turned him down. The 'insult' might have rankled. If

Tony were looking for a murderer among the people he knew in Wallingham, McNaughton measured up as well as most people.

Had they gone straight back to the McNaughton home?

Tony walked along to the nearest telephone kiosk, hung about for five minutes, and then went inside and called the McNaughton number. The couple had had ample time to get back.

Mrs McNaughton answered, in a blaze of sound.

'Is Mrs Denton there?' Tony didn't try to disguise his voice.

'No, young Tony Grey, she's not. I don't know where she is. She went to see that impossible man, Swanley, and she hasn't come back. I shall send Pat round to talk to him if she doesn't turn up soon, but never mind *her*. What about your Sarah? What are you going to do? It's preposterous, Swanley ought not to be trusted to patrol a street. Do you want any help?'

'No – '

'Money?' barked Mrs McNaughton. 'You needn't be shy, I know you haven't much, can't have or you wouldn't live in that barn of a house. Let me help. But don't make any mistake,' she roared on, compelling him to remove the receiver an inch from his ear, 'it isn't for your sake or for Sarah's, she's asked for trouble. This will probably do her good, it'll teach her that she isn't almighty. But I'd spend my last penny on making Swanley look a fool.'

'If I need money, I'll come and see you,' Tony said. 'Thanks very much. 'Bye.' He put the receiver down before she could speak again, and rubbed his ear. There was something about Mrs McNaughton which it was hard to resist. When he stepped out of the booth, he was smiling faintly.

He walked along to the Rose & Crown. Jameson and several other newspapermen were in the bar. He managed to catch Jameson's eye without being seen by the others, and Jameson joined him in the hall, a few minutes later.

'What's the news of importance?' Tony demanded.

'Just a whisper, old chap, that the jewels in this show are

worth a fortune. Really big stuff. Ever been in the stolen jewellery business?'

'Not yet,' said Tony. The news was hardly sensational, but was undoubtedly significant. 'Will you do a hush-hush job for me?'

'What is it?'

'Go round to Mrs McNaughton, and find out whether her son Pat's at home. Also, whether Mrs Denton is still there. And if they're not, find out where they are.'

Jameson looked at him out of eyes both keen and shrewd. '*Mrs* Denton,' he said lightly.

'I know the truth about that, but I don't know what she's doing with Pat McNaughton tonight, and I think it might be worth finding out.'

'Big, handsome, hearty,' mused Jameson, 'rather like Denton was himself. Hard-faced, beneath his genial exterior. Like his mother, just a lot of noise – or isn't he? What do you know?'

'I'm guessing.'

'I'll see what I can find out. Where will you be?'

'At home.'

'I hope you've some whisky,' Jameson said.

He arrived at the Middle Street house, by car, half-an-hour after Tony had reached home, and finished a snack meal. For a London reporter, he was showing some signs of excitement.

'They're out at a wayside pub, other side of Hoodle,' he said. 'Dining together, according to Ma. They telephoned to say so. Care to come out and see what it's all about?'

'Hadn't you better go yourself?'

'Your trouble is diffidence,' Jameson said. 'Life must be taken by the throat or you'll die of ennui. Coming?'

He had a roomy Buick with a fine turn of speed, and was an expert driver. They crossed the bridge and swung on to the Hoodle Road.

'What made you begin to wonder about this pair, Grey?'

'Off the record?'

'Yes.'

'She came to see me, and he was hiding in another garden. I couldn't understand why. She seemed to cheer up remarkably, too, I wondered if she were quite so cut up as she made out. I may be all wrong, but –'

'If I make one good guess in ten, I think myself lucky,' Jameson said. 'Do you know this road?'

'Not really well.'

'Pity. Mrs Mac gave me the name of the pub, the Corner Inn. The landlord of the Rose & Crown told me where to find it. Ten miles on the other side of Hoodle, and on a hairpin bend. Apparently they do a good trade in brandy, after accidents.'

'I haven't any money to spare for brandy,' Tony said, 'take it easy on the corners.'

Jameson laughed, and his foot went down harder on the accelerator. The headlights carved a great channel of light out of the night, shone on telegraph poles which glistened like silver, on hedges and on overhanging trees and, long before Tony had expected to, came upon an S bend, with the words: *'Dangerous Corner'*.

'This must be it,' Jameson said, and slowed down.

They pulled up on the car park, and climbed out. Jameson stood looking at the other cars.

Tony said: 'Aren't we in a hurry?'

'Not for a minute,' said Jameson, softly. 'Isn't that an Austin 20? And doesn't Superintendent Swanley drive one? What's his number?'

'I don't know –'

'I do. WAL 1122,' Jameson crooned, 'and this is it. You're not the only one with a hunch, chum, you may have suspected better than you knew! Nice little job over there,' he added, and then his voice sharpened. 'You seem to know it.'

Tony was looking at a glistening Sunbeam Talbot; at Rick Asterley's car.

CHAPTER 22

Quiet Dinner

They moved away from the car park, Jameson looking curiously at Tony, who made no comment. The head and shoulders of a man showed up against a lighted window; it was one of Swanley's sergeants. Another man, the bright young constable, stood unobtrusively in the shadows near the door. Jameson chuckled.

'Taking names of all who enter here,' he said.

'That puts me on the suspect list again,' said Tony.

'You're used to that, aren't you?' They stood in a brightly-lit hall, where a log fire blazed. 'Doesn't seem to be anyone about, does there?'

A murmur of voices came from a door marked 'Cocktail Bar'. A wide passage in front of them had several signs sticking out above the doors, including 'Dining Room' and 'Lounge'. In one corner of the hall was a small office, with a reception desk; a portly woman appeared at it, suddenly.

'Can I help you, gentlemen?'

'We can get dinner here, can't we?' asked Jameson.

'Yes, sir – third door on the right.' She gave a bright smile, and promptly disappeared.

Jameson led the way towards the dining-room, glancing quickly through the door of the lounge as he passed; several people were sitting there but no one whom Tony knew. A narrow, adjacent door was marked 'Private'. Jameson opened this, and Tony caught a glimpse of Pat McNaughton and Anne Denton.

'Well, well,' Jameson drawled.

They passed on to the smoking-room, and here they pushed the door open with a bang.

Swanley and shorthand writer Bennett sat at a table close to the wall. Swanley started to his feet. Jameson waved cheerfully.

'Nice work. Look who's here!' He poked a thumb over his shoulder towards Tony. 'He's in good company tonight, though, just on a mission of inquiry. Want us?'

Swanley shook his head.

Jameson withdrew.

He said suddenly, unexpectedly: 'What shook you outside, by the way? Whose car did you recognise?'

'A friend's.'

'Come clean,' said Jameson. 'Aren't I being helpful?'

'Were McNaughton and Mrs Denton alone?'

'Yes.'

'We'd better have a look in here, then,' Tony said, leading the way into the dining-room.

The room was crowded; it was impossible to see all those present at a single glance. Tony stood by the wall, looking round as if for a vacant table, actually for Asterley.

The police-surgeon was at the far end of the room, at a table by himself. He looked up, startled, and then began to smile.

A waitress came up.

'I'm sorry, sir, but we'll have to keep you waiting for a few minutes, would you mind –'

Asterley was beckoning.

'There's a friend of mine at that end table,' Tony said. 'We'll go there.'

He threaded his way towards the police-surgeon, with Jameson behind him.

Asterley waved a welcoming hand.

'Hallo, Tony. What are you doing out here?'

'I thought a change from Wallingham would be a good idea,' said Tony. 'This is Mr Jameson – Dr Asterley. Can we share your table?'

'I'd be offended if you didn't.' Asterley grinned. 'Isn't Mr Jameson from the Press?'

'No privacy in my life,' said Jameson sadly. 'Press Association, yes.'

They sat down. Asterley's empty soup plate was in front of him, so he hadn't started dinner long.

'What's really brought you, Tony?' Asterley was as friendly as ever. 'McNaughton and Mrs Denton?'

'Yes.'

'The same bait brought me.' Asterley lowered his voice. 'I'm in an almost desperate mood. I can see this case building up against Sarah, and I don't think she did it. That's about your own angle, isn't it?'

'Yes,' Tony said shortly.

'Where there is beauty, there must be innocence,' Jameson said dryly. 'Anything for the Press, Dr Asterley?'

'Most emphatically not. And don't forget there is a law of libel.'

A waitress came up, and they gave their order. When she'd gone, Asterley said:

'I suppose we can trust Mr Jameson, Tony?'

'With your life,' Jameson declared. 'All is off the record until I give the word.' He spoke soberly. 'Of course I'm after a story, but mostly I'd like to be in at the kill. I don't think Swanley has made his final pounce, yet.'

'Any reason for saying that?' Asterley's voice was sharp.

'Hunch,' Jameson assured him.

'I hope it's a good one. I was in difficulties almost from the beginning of this case, Tony, because I was near the common on that unpleasant afternoon.' He smiled at Tony's look of surprise. 'You're not the only one shaken by that! Swanley knew it, and I think he's developed a theory that I saw something I didn't pass on.'

'Did you?'

Jameson was looking at the police-surgeon intently.

'No. I don't have to pass on rumours that might possibly have some bearing on a case, until I'm pretty sure that they're important. I was told that McNaughton's car was parked among some trees, and didn't tell Swanley. My informant did, and also mentioned that he'd told me. Ah, here's the roast beef.'

'Well, well!' breathed Jameson. 'Weren't you the bird who sent Mrs Denton to Mrs McNaughton?'

'I was indeed. I thus made sure that while keeping an eye on Mrs Denton, the police had to keep one on the McNaughtons. Swanley's only just woken up to the fact that young McNaughton and the Dentons were acquainted before. Since I had that jolt – mild suspicions by the police – I've kept my eyes open, and learned that McNaughton and Mrs Denton were coming here. When Swanley followed them and found me waiting, he went off the handle. Poor old Tom! It's the first time he and I have had a sharp difference since I was appointed police-surgeon. I think he thinks I'm waiting to confer with the other two.'

He helped himself liberally to potatoes and cauliflower.

'Aren't you?' asked Jameson mildly.

Asterley chuckled. 'No. I don't quite know what I should have done on my own, but as Swanley's here, there's no need to do anything. I can enjoy my dinner without worrying about it. What did you hope to do, Tony?'

'Find out why they came here.'

'You can leave that to Swanley, too. Interesting that McNaughton and Mrs Denton are in a private room, isn't it?' Asterley asked. 'What can they have to discuss that's as private as that? Something odd about them, isn't there? I've always thought that Swanley might be wise to find out more about Mrs Denton. She's a strange young woman with some fixed purpose – but I don't know what that is. I suppose Swanley has searched her rooms at Hoodle? Any idea, Tony?'

'No.'

'You know,' said Jameson, in a thoughtful voice, 'we might be wasting our time. We might be doing better if we were at Mrs Denton's place in Hoodle. Swanley might have messed some things up, but he isn't a fool. He'll probably have Mrs Denton's place watched, so the fun might start there.'

'Ah,' said Asterley. 'If I were a newspaperman, I'd be in Hoodle tonight.'

Jameson finished his soup.

'I think I dare wait for the roast beef,' he said thoughtfully. 'Coming with me, Tony?'

'Be careful,' Asterley said. 'Even Swanley won't suspect a journalist of having part in this murder, but he might wonder if you go on to Mrs Denton's place, Tony. I'd keep out of it, if I were you.'

'Please yourself,' Jameson said casually. 'Ah, here comes the food.'

They both rose to leave, half-an-hour later.

There was a hatch in the wall of the smoking-room of the Corner Inn, opening through to the little room which was occasionally used for small private dinner parties. It was an insignificant-looking little hatch, rarely noticed. Bennett was writing furiously at one side of it, while Swanley listened intently. The hatch was open a little, not enough to be marked by the couple in the other room, but sufficient to allow their voices to travel clearly.

Bennett had taken down everything he had heard; little had been of importance, until Anne Denton had said in a strained voice:

'I wonder how long they'll be.'

'Not long,' McNaughton assured her. 'You worry too much, my sweet – that's always been your trouble. You worried too much about Ray.'

'Heaven knows, I had reason!'

'But has it helped?' McNaughton asked. 'This chap wants to see you here, and he won't expect you to have company. He should get a nasty shock, when he arrives.' He laughed, and there was a pause, enabling Bennett to ease his cramped fingers.

Swanley, looking rested but alert, glanced towards the door. This was the second reference to the fact that the couple expected a visitor. Asterley and Tony Grey were here, either might be the man expected. Swanley was still smarting from the quarrel with Asterley, doubtful whether he was justified in his suspicions, distressed about the possibility.

He lit a cigarette.

'Anne,' McNaughton said, suddenly, and there was a different note in his voice.

'Yes.'

'I know it's been hell for you, but – it'll pass. We'll get through safely, and there's a future.' McNaughton's voice was pitched low. 'You can't be blamed because Ray sold you a dummy. *I'll* never hold it against you. I know it's a hell of a time to talk of this, but can't you and I – '

A sharp report cut across his words; and after it came a short, tense silence. A chair crashed, something fell from a table, and broke; and then Anne screamed.

Swanley rushed to the door, and as he did so, Anne screamed again.

McNaughton lay sprawled across the table, a brilliant crimson splash staining the snow white tablecloth. The window was smashed. Outside, men were shouting. Staring at McNaughton with horror in her rounded eyes, stood Anne Denton, absolutely still.

Swanley sprang to the window.

A man passed; Asterley, running fast. Almost on his heels came Tony Grey. There was a third man nearby, but Swanley could not see him clearly. Others were running in the distance, and a man was shouting. Someone else rushed into the room, as Swanley flung the broken window up and climbed through.

CHAPTER 23

More Murder?

Tony and the others heard the shot as they reached the garden, saw the light shining from the window of the private room, and the man standing near it. They heard Anne scream.

Jameson shouted.

The man at the window turned and ran. The others dashed after him, Asterley easily in the lead. The darkness was swallowing up the man with the gun, who had run through the flower garden towards the vegetable patch at the back. Tony wasn't familiar with this place, but Asterley seemed to know exactly what he was doing, where he was going. He passed through a gap in a beech hedge, and suddenly the others saw the man with the gun, a silhouette against the sky as he climbed the brick wall which surrounded the garden.

There was a vivid flash and a loud report. A bullet smacked into the ground near Tony. He heard Asterley gasp, saw him stagger. The man at the top of the wall fired again.

The path was smooth and hard, good for running. Tony saw the wall, made a running jump, and clutched the top of it. He hung there for a moment, then hauled himself up, and sprang to the ground. Another shot flashed, the bullet smacking against the bricks. He landed lightly. The man in front was only a shadowy figure now, running across open meadowland. He seemed to be heading for the road. Jameson called out a warning, but Tony raced on, grimly, obstinately. He believed he was drawing nearer. The other stumbled.

Tony saw the head and shoulders drop, the silhouette against the starlit sky almost disappear, then staggeringly, appear again. Intuitively, Tony flung himself to one side. This time the flash and roar were nearer, revealing for a split second the broad nose of the man who had attacked him in Wallingham.

The fugitive was about ten feet away, gun in hand.

Tony saw a hedge loom up, the man lost against it; he judged where he thought the man was, and leapt forward in a flying tackle. He clutched at a leg, but his fingers missed the man's ankle. He thought of the gun pointing down at him, and clutched again.

The roar was deafening, the flash almost blinding him. But he'd thrown the man off his balance, heard him crash against the hedge, and – he himself wasn't hurt. He hit out savagely. He heard a gasp, as of pain, let go and flung himself bodily on to the man. He hurt his right hand against something hard; the gun. The hot breath of his victim was on his face, and he jerked his head down, groping for the man's neck.

This was undoubtedly the man who had smashed his head against the pavement.

There was murder in Tony's mind, a savage anger that took complete possession of him. He felt the man desperately struggling for breath.

Then Jameson's voice cut in sharply: 'Enough. I've got the gun.'

Tony held on.

Jameson snapped: 'Enough!' and struck him on the side of the head, just severely enough to make him let go. He rolled to one side, gasping for breath. He was aware of others drawing up, and of men's voices, was unable to think for a few seconds, hardly able to feel. He knew that someone was bending over him, and felt a hand at his face. Someone else asked:

'Is he hurt?'

'We'll soon see. Better get some light.'

'Go round to the road, bring a car along, and switch the

headlights on.' That was Swanley. 'Drive into the field, if you can.'

'Yes, sir.'

Tony tried to sit up, but firm hands pressed him down.

He was not hurt, apart from bruises and scratches. The headlights of the car which had been brought into the field shone on the man he had caught, sitting against the hedge, collar and tie off, his face looking ghastly in the powerful light.

Swanley was standing over him; so was Bennett and a small group of policemen. Jameson wasn't in sight.

'All right,' Swanley said, 'get him away.'

'To the pub, sir?'

'Have Dr Asterley look him over, and if he's all right take him into Wallingham. Have him watched closely.'

'Right, sir.'

Two men helped the gunman to his feet. He made no protest. They took his arms and they walked off towards the inn, where lights were shining at every window.

Swanley came across to Tony.

'Wasn't Asterley hurt?' Tony asked sharply.

'Not badly,' said Swanley. 'A slight wound in the shoulder. You seem to have had a lucky escape, Mr Grey.'

'It's a good thing he couldn't shoot straight.' The question which was hovering in Tony's mind came out abruptly. 'How is McNaughton?'

'I don't know. He's on the way to hospital, and was unconscious when he left here.'

'Mrs – Denton?'

Swanley said: 'I don't think she was hurt. Can you walk back?'

'Yes.'

'Drive the car to the parking place again,' Swanley instructed one of the several men who were still about, and started off with Tony to the inn. They reached a gate in the garden wall, in silence, and then Swanley said: 'What made you come out to this inn, Mr Grey?'

'Mrs Denton came to see me, and I found her manner puzzling. I went to see if she met anyone outside, and saw her driving off with McNaughton. His car had been parked rather furtively in an empty house, and – ' Tony shrugged. 'I came out here with a reporter.'

'Why didn't you inform me?'

'I didn't see that it would do any good. I knew nothing. After all,' Tony said heavily, 'if you were interested in them, I knew you'd have them watched. I wasn't sure whether you were interested.' Swanley made no comment, and Tony went on: 'Will you release Miss Mellison tonight?'

'That is most unlikely,' Swanley said. 'Have you seen the man before?'

'He attacked me, the other night.'

'On the tow-path?'

'No, the first attack.'

'Are you sure?'

'He has the same broad nose, and I'm pretty sure. It could have been someone like him, but – ' Tony broke off.

'Well, we've got him for tonight's job, anyhow,' Swanley said. 'Are you sure you'd never seen him before the first attack?'

'If you still think I know anything about this, you're crazier than I thought you were!'

They were within range of the light from the inn, and Swanley actually smiled.

'I should hate you to have a worse opinion of my methods than the one you have already so exhaustively explained to me.' The tone of his voice was lighter, he was more like the man whom Tony had first seen, on the common. 'Had you any previous reason to believe that Mr McNaughton and Mrs Denton knew each other? Or that McNaughton knew Denton?'

'No.'

'Thanks,' said Swanley, and they reached the back door. 'I'll want to see you again later, and I'll send a car round for you. You'll go straight back to Wallingham, I hope.'

'Yes,' Tony said, and forgot for the moment that he was dependent on Jameson for transport.

The lounge had been emptied of the hotel guests. As they reached it, the prisoner was being led out, between two detectives. He looked at the floor all the time, and shuffled his feet; once, he fingered his throat, and Tony saw the bruising marked on it. If Jameson hadn't arrived, he might have choked the man to death.

Asterley and Jameson were in the lounge, with Bennett.

'Hallo, Tony!' Asterley was sitting on the arm of a chair, with his coat slung over a bandaged shoulder. 'Jameson tells me your photograph is about to appear again under the headlines: "Fearless lover risks life catching a gunman".'

'Forget it,' Tony said, abruptly.

Jameson finished his whisky and rang for another.

'I'm driving you both back,' he said. 'You look all in, Tony – sit back and take it easy. You've done more than your share in the night's good work.'

Tony said: 'Forget that, too. Where's Mrs Denton?'

'She's going to my place,' said Asterley. 'I've telephoned Dora, who'll have a room ready for her. Suffering from shock, of course, and she must have a good night's sleep. If you really mean, has she said anything, I don't know. I'm not likely to, either. Although I'm friends again with Swanley, I don't think he'll confide in me until this is over.'

'I've picked up some odds and ends,' said Jameson, hopefully. 'That McNaughton and Mrs Denton are expecting a visitor, and Swanley probably thought that one of you, or both, fitted the bill. You know, there are still quite a few mysteries to clear up. Who did the man want to kill – McNaughton or the girl? And did he kill Denton, or is the killer still footloose?'

Asterley said: 'I'm empty of ideas. Tom Swanley is right enough in this, that it's no time for guessing. Finish your drink and take me home, will you?'

Tony, arrayed in a dressing-gown, sat back in an armchair in his study, seven morning newspapers spread out on the floor round his feet, the eighth on his lap. Jameson, looking fresh and cheerful, sat on a corner of the table, swinging his legs and smoking a cigarette.

It was half past nine; Tony had been up for half an hour, and Jameson had arrived ten minutes later, with most of the newspapers. Having exhausted the headlines he was itemising the small print.

'Mrs Denton slept well, under a sleeping draught, and is still asleep. A policewoman spent the night in the room with her. McNaughton was operated on during the night, they took the bullet out of his head, but it's touch and go – not a second murder yet, but pretty close to it. McNaughton's room has been pretty thoroughly searched, Mrs McNaughton is silenced for once. Whether Swanley found anything, I don't know. The landlady at Hoodle didn't think much of it when the police searched Mrs Denton's room last night. Again, I don't know whether they found anything. Probably, yes, because Swanley is chirpy, and he hasn't been very bright and lively over this affair before. That's not bad, for a start – I'll go and make the tea.'

Tony had put a kettle on, just before the reporter arrived; it was probably boiling furiously. He watched Jameson go out, swaggering slightly, amiable and friendly as ever. The man whistled as he went along the passage. The sound faded, and there was silence. Photographs of himself stared up at him from the newspapers; the story was on every front page. He picked up one, and read:

> 'The police have reason to believe that the gunman, Charles Hollen, is one of a gang of jewel thieves which has operated on both sides of the Channel during the past few years. It is already known that Raymond Denton was in touch with this gang. The police have been on the trail for a long time, and further developments can be expected hourly.'

But Sarah was still under arrest; still charged with Denton's murder. Why? Wasn't there evidence, now, that she had nothing to do with it? Or was the mystery of the stolen jewels, in her possession, evidence that she had something to do with the crimes? Who had given her those jewels? She'd been on the point of telling Swanley, when Tony had stopped her. Swanley knew, presumably; Swanley had known or guessed much more than he'd ever allowed anyone to think – had even suspected Asterley!

Tony smiled.

Jameson came in, with the tea.

'Now what's funny?' he asked. 'Think you're right out of the wood?'

'Just hoping,' said Tony. 'Surely you don't think that Swanley believes –'

'There's no telling, with policemen,' Jameson said. 'Now you're wide awake, you can look at some facts. More than one man has been involved in this case, and only one has been caught. What's more, he attacked you – and there's only your word for it that he was after something he thought you had. I wouldn't be over confident, if I were you. That prisoner could damn you, Tony.'

'Nonsense! He –'

'Oh, not only with the truth. With lies. Remember, there's still a possibility that another nasty customer lurks in Wallingham. It could be someone pretty highly placed in this jewel racket. It's possible that Hollen will lie to protect the real rogue, and – ' he shrugged. 'Milk and sugar?'

Tony said: 'It would be fantastic!'

'Well, I don't know,' said Jameson, pouring out with a steady hand. 'There's one little piece of information I didn't give you, and everyone forgot to tell you last night. Considerate people, aren't we? Mrs Denton said one or two things, before she was taken away from the pub. Among them – that she was expecting to see you there.'

Tony gasped.

'Shattering, but true,' said Jameson. 'What's more, my son, she came to see you because she and McNaughton had hatched a little plot, between them. Before she came, she'd had a message, telling her to go to the Corner Inn. She suspected that the message came from you. She came round, to see if she could get anything out of you, and funked the questions. McNaughton, lurking nearby, was simply acting the gallant, she says. Apparently he had no confidence in Swanley, either. The story is that they were expecting you. And you went there! Also – ' Jameson brought over a cup of steaming tea – 'it *is* conceivable that you framed Hollen, isn't it? Lured him there, and having done that, caught him and turned yourself into a hero. Don't blame me for this somewhat fantastic idea – it's quite a popular one, at the moment.'

CHAPTER 24

Fresh Suspicion

Jameson sipped his tea; Tony didn't touch his, but stared at the newspaperman while he absorbed these new factors. It wasn't any use rejecting them, or calling them nonsense; there was cold logic in the story, sufficient to make Jameson thoughtful; and if he were half inclined to think it true, Swanley probably went the whole hog.

'Drink up,' said Jameson. 'I – hallo, visitors.' He heard a car turn into the drive, and looked towards the window. 'Shall I let them in on my way out?'

'Will you,' Tony said listlessly.

'All is not yet lost,' said Jameson.

He grinned as he disappeared round the door.

There was a ring at the front door bell, and then a man said:

'Is Mr Grey in?' It was not Swanley.

'Sure,' said Jameson, laconically. 'I don't know whether he's anxious to receive visitors, but I'll see.'

'I must see him,' the man said. He had a deep, mellow voice, which Tony hadn't heard before. 'Don't announce us – which room is it?'

'Us?'

There was a pause.

Tony stood up, and the newspaper slithered from his lap. He put the cup down on a small table, and turned towards the door as it opened. A tall, distinguished looking man came in.

Behind him, was Sarah.

*

She looked tired, but lovely. She came forward slowly, hands outstretched; she always seemed to greet him like that. There was no impulsiveness about it now, she approached hesitantly, and her eyes asked questions.

Tony said : 'Sarah,' in a husky voice.

Next moment she was in his arms. He didn't know how long they stayed like that, but at last she drew back. Jameson was in the doorway, grinning. The older man stood gravely by the table.

Sarah took his hand.

'Tony, this is my father.'

'And I'm very glad to meet you,' said Mellison. 'I arrived last night, and was able to see Sarah. She told me what a help you've been. I'll be able to stay "thank you" some other time.'

'You'll never be able to say it properly,' Sarah said.

'When did they release you?' Tony demanded happily, all that Jameson had drummed into him driven clean out of his mind.

'This morning.'

'I brought a legal friend with me from London, and after what happened last night, he was able to persuade the police that there was no excuse for holding Sarah any longer,' Mellison explained. 'Sarah refused to go home until she'd been to see you. Will you come with us? Or follow us, as soon as you're ready? We'll be more than happy, and you'll have a great deal to talk about.'

'Do, Tony,' Sarah pleaded.

He began to recall what Jameson had said.

'You'll be more than welcome,' insisted Mellison.

'Well – ' Tony hesitated. 'I haven't heard from Swanley this morning. He wants to see me. When I've finished with him, I'll – be delighted to come.' The word 'delighted' was lame and inadequate, but he couldn't get his mind clear. 'Sarah, it's magnificent to have you free. Wonderful!'

'There were moments when I almost felt that they'd prove I was guilty,' Sarah said, and went on softly : 'Tony,

I didn't kill Denton, you know. You believe that. don't you?'

'Of course I believe it! Obviously the police have come round to that, too.' He laughed, suddenly, wildly gay. 'I'll go and see Swanley, not wait for him, and get up to your house as soon as I can. Thanks for bringing her, Mr Mellison!'

Mellison smiled.

'You'll probably live to learn that if Sarah wants to do a thing, she does it, no matter who else has to help. Sarah, we ought to go, your mother will be getting anxious. Yes, we both flew back from Paris,' he added. 'You'll be up to luncheon, then?'

Tony said: 'Yes, thanks very much,' and went to the door with them.

Mellison drove a Daimler. It purred out of the drive, sleek and imposing. Sarah waved through the window as they disappeared.

Tony turned back to the study, bewildered but with a sense of growing exultation. Once, he laughed aloud. He found himself grinning into the mirror, as he shaved. All that Jameson had said seemed so much froth, there couldn't be anything serious in it. Why on earth should Anne Denton have named him? It *was* fantastic to think that the prisoner might do the same.

The mood lasted until he was ready to go out. The sooner he saw Swanley, the better; probably Jameson had exaggerated. Tony was prepared to believe that everything would go smoothly from now on. Sarah was free; *Sarah*. He was in love with her, he knew that now.

Sarah was free! He was near the front door, already making up his mind how to start with Swanley, when the front door bell rang.

The police?

He felt a moment's alarm, brushed the thought aside, opened the door and was confronted by Mrs McNaughton.

She looked old, raddled, despairing. Her eyes held the pathos of a wounded animal as she gazed at him, without speaking.

'I want to see you,' she said at last.

He stood aside and she came in, her usual exuberance and vitality muted.

'What is it, Mrs McNaughton?'

She looked at him for a long time, without speaking, and as if willing him to silence. Then:

'What has my son done to you?'

'Nothing at all! I –'

'Then why did you do it?' she asked, wearily. 'Why did you plan to kill him?'

'You're quite wrong. I caught –'

'Oh, yes, you caught the man who actually fired the shot,' said Mrs McNaughton, 'but you sent him. I know everything now.' She continued to look at him with eyes which had been dull, but now glistened with a strange light. 'He's all I've got, and – you tried to kill him.'

'Mrs McNaughton –'

'You murderer, why did you do it?'

'Don't be silly,' Tony said sharply. 'I know nothing about it. I caught the man who shot him, isn't that proof enough?'

'No,' said Mrs McNaughton, 'it isn't proof at all. I was afraid it was you. I don't know why, but I had a feeling all along. I didn't like you. I tried to be friendly, and you rebuffed me. I knew he was mixed up in some – folly. I didn't know what it was, or who it was. Now I know.'

'Mrs McNaughton –'

'Be quiet!' she shouted. 'I tell you, I know the truth. I heard them talking. He was sorry for Anne, I'm not sure that he isn't in love with her. He took to her from the moment she came into the house. He had – he has such a wonderful big heart. He'd make her a good husband if he once settled down. I tell you I heard them talking!'

She shouted again; the sharp switch from a whispering voice to one of maniacal fury, was somehow frightening, terrifying in its abnormality.

'All right,' Tony said, 'What did they say?'

'She'd had a telephone message, telling her to meet a man at the Corner Inn. She thought it was your voice. She told my boy that, and he said he'd go with her. She didn't want to go alone, poor child. She was frightened out of her wits, and Pat said he'd go, he would always dare anything. They expected to see you there, and instead – you sent an assassin, the devil who tried to kill my son. *Why did you do it?*' She screeched the words as she lumbered to her feet, her right hand behind her, holding – what?

'I sent no one. Mrs McNaughton, if you'll listen to reason –'

'To lies, you mean,' she spat at him. 'Lies, lies, lies, they spill out of you! Do you think I don't know when a man's *lying*. Stay where you are!' She was breathing heavily now, and trembling; and the right hand was still hidden, behind her back. '*Why did you do it?* What devilry did you get him mixed up in? Out with it! And if you don't –' she dropped her voice again. 'And if you don't, I'll shoot you dead.'

She swung her arm round, and covered him with a gun.

She was only a few feet away from him, quivering, stocky, full of hate. Her finger, fat, deadly, diamond encrusted, was on the trigger.

Tony, cold as ice, stood absolutely still.

'*Tell me why you did it, what you made him do?*'

If he denied it again, she might shoot. Whatever he said, that might happen.

'*Answer me!*' she shrieked.

'All right,' said Tony, as if wearily, 'all right, I'll tell you.' He put his hand to his pocket, hardly daring to move; fingering his tobacco pouch. It was three parts full, and fairly heavy.

'Hurry!'

'I went to the inn to see him,' began Tony, 'because I thought that he could help –'

Suddenly he flung the tobacco pouch straight into her face. Her head jerked sharply to one side. He leapt, swinging his arm round, clutching her wrist.

The gun went off, the roar deafening him. He had her

wrist held tightly, and he twisted; the gun dropped. He kicked it along the carpet, beneath the table. Then he let her go and backed away, but she hadn't finished yet.

She hurled herself at him, two hundred pounds of solid flesh, and he couldn't dodge.

CHAPTER 25

The Lies Of A Lady

Tony fended her off, but not until she had drawn blood from his cheeks. She was about to attack again when the door swung violently open and one of Swanley's men appeared.

'What – ' he began, and then darted forward. Competently, authoritatively, he guided her to a chair. She lay there in a state of total collapse, her eyes closed, her great flailing limbs stilled to all but a restless twitching as the detective bent down and groped for the gun.

Another appeared in the doorway.

'How did you get in?' Tony asked, holding his handkerchief to his face.

'We had a key, sir – after the burglary here, you let us have one, remember?' The man, vaguely familiar, was polite and unflurried, although his companion crawled from beneath the table, looking flushed and embarrassed, but with the gun in his hand. 'Would you mind telling us what happened?'

'Weren't you listening at the window?'

'We couldn't catch everything, sir.'

'You caught all you're going to, from me,' growled Tony. 'Mrs McNaughton seems to think that I was responsible for the attack on her son, and – '

Mrs McNaughton buried her face in her hands, and leaned forward, rocking herself to and fro in the age-old gesture of despair. Tony looked from her to the detective, then abruptly turned round and went out.

There was a policeman outside, who made no attempt to stop him. Tony reached the main road, and heard a car horn blare out, glanced across and recognised Jameson's Buick.

Jameson pulled up.

'Going places?'

'To see Swanley. Can you give me a lift?'

'Any time,' said Jameson, and Tony climbed in. 'You look as if you've had a fight.'

'I have.'

'Any news?'

'Off the record, Mrs McNaughton has the same fool idea as you, apparently. How is her son?'

'I've just left the hospital, and the report's fairly encouraging.'

Tony dabbed gingerly at his cheek, and contrived to bring some sort of law and order into his face before they reached the police station.

'Thanks,' he said. 'I shouldn't wait. Swanley will probably throw his weight about again.'

Jameson chuckled.

'You're evenly matched,' he said, and switched off the engine. 'I'll wait.'

Tony ran up the shallow stairs to Swanley's room. He reached the door, knocked on it, and went in without waiting for an answer. Swanley was alone.

He dropped his pen.

'Who said – '

'I said,' growled Tony. 'I'm sick to death of this show. Did Mrs Denton say I was going to meet her at the Corner Inn, or didn't she?'

Swanley said: 'Mr Grey – '

'Did she or didn't she?' Tony stepped to the desk, and leaned against it, glaring down. 'Mrs McNaughton says so. Jameson says so. Is it the truth, or a silly lie you've been spreading round? And what about Hollen? Has he damned me yet – or are you telling him what to say, so that you can put me under arrest?'

Swanley picked up his pen.

'Sit down, Mr Grey, please. Yes, Mrs Denton did think you had asked her to meet you.'

'Well, I didn't.'

'She wasn't sure.' Swanley was remarkably mild, even soothing, and Tony found himself sitting down, and even pulling the chair nearer the desk. 'As for Hollen – he has made a statement, Mr Grey, and a most interesting one. There are parts of it which I can tell you.' He flipped over several pages of typewritten matter in front of him, and went on: 'He is a thief with a long record of violence, and if you read the newspapers, you know that he's connected with a gang of rogues who deal in stolen and smuggled jewels. *Do* you read the newspapers?'

'I read that.'

'What the newspapers don't yet know, but soon will, is that he has admitted that he made frequent visits to Wallingham, because one of the fences – the buyers of stolen jewels – lived here. That is the man Denton came to see, among others. According to Hollen, Mrs Denton was not concerned. There were several centres in England which Denton and Hollen had to visit, to sell their goods, and in many of them Denton made friends with attractive young women. It appears to have been Mrs Denton's misfortune that he selected her, in Wallingham.'

Tony said: 'Well, where do I come in?'

'I don't yet know,' said Swanley, with apparent frankness. 'It is now established that Mrs Denton was acquainted with Mr McNaughton. They had met two or three times. Mr McNaughton saw her on the afternoon of the murder, and talked to her before she cycled across the common. According to her, it was a chance meeting.'

'Or is that what they wanted you to believe?' demanded Tony.

'I don't know,' said Swanley, and smiled again. He had recovered his poise, and seemed rested and much more composed. 'Several people obviously want me to believe what isn't true. I –' The telephone bell rang. 'Sorry, I must answer this.' He took off the receiver, and began to make notes on a pad in front of him; he spoke only three times in as many minutes, then said: 'Yes, I have all that, goodbye.' He put down the pencil and looked across at Tony. 'That was from the man who interrupted the scene between you and Mrs McNaughton. Where was I? Oh, yes, Mrs Denton was going to meet her husband, who had probably come to Wallingham on his usual business, to sell stolen or smuggled stones. His murderer was, in all probability, a customer, who was afraid of being given away.'

'So it could have been McNaughton. Mrs McNaughton –'

'Was sure that someone had been leading her son astray,' murmured Swanley, and his smile suggested the absurdity of thinking that a strong-willed, aggressive man of McNaughton's temper could be led astray. 'Yes, he could have been the customer, of course, and you won't need telling that he might have befriended Mrs Denton in order to find out what she knew and who was coming to see her. We don't yet know. We do know that Denton had ten thousand pounds worth of precious stones in his possession when he arrived in Wallingham, and they were gone when his body was found.'

'Who told you?'

'Hollen. The evidence is pretty strong, Mr Grey. We have Hollen's companion under arrest, and know everything except the identity of Denton's murderer.'

'*Every*thing?'

'I think so, yes. I don't yet know who sent you that diamond – but Denton was one of a highly organised ring, dealing in stolen jewels and other forms of criminality. When he came here, Denton had the jewels and a small notebook, containing damning evidence against the leader and members of the organisation – in short, an address book with lists of customers, details of jewels on offer. It was not found on Denton's body.'

Tony said: 'Didn't you find it?'

'No. As the people concerned were not molested by the police, the London leader was sure we hadn't taken it. So, you and Mrs Denton were suspected – as murderers who now had a stranglehold on a powerful criminal ring. Both of you were attacked, in an effort to find both the jewels and the book.

'Later, suspicion switched to you and Miss Mellison. You were attacked on the river. You were sent that diamond, as a bribe to keep quiet. Miss Mellison was sent the anonymous letter to harass and unnerve her – as it did.'

'But why attack McNaughton as well? Why get Mrs Denton to that pub?'

Swanley was almost urbane.

'Remember, the people in London were certain of nothing – and in hourly fear of disaster. Your behaviour finally convinced them that you were not involved. They switched back to Mrs Denton, as an obvious suspect. They told her to go to the Corner Inn. McNaughton went with her and together they made another possible, in fact probable, pair of accomplices. By then, Hollen and his superiors were desperately anxious to get the notebook. It was now fairly clear that you weren't involved; you and Miss Mellison were paired. The other pair met at the Corner Inn, and the shooting was an attempt to frighten. Hollen says McNaughton moved into the line of fire. He says that he – and his accomplices – did not kill Denton or take that book.'

Tony said: 'I see. McNaughton –'

'He appears to have been befriending Mrs Denton. Now, what is this about Mrs McNaughton's visit?'

Tony went into some detail.

'Hmm. I'd say that she wanted to frighten you into making a confession. She is passionately fond of her son, and his danger affected her very badly. Well now – I think you can help us find the murderer.'

'Oh, do you,' said Tony. 'I don't know whether I can, and don't see why I should.'

'Don't you?' Swanley took something from the desk and held it out.

Tony took it, and saw that it was a photograph of Sarah, at her most vivid and loveliest. He looked sharply into Swanley's eyes.

'Haven't you released her?'

'We have, Mr Grey. Now – ' Swanley stood up, and came round the desk, stood looking down, grave-faced, in sober earnest. 'We are also quite sure that Miss Mellison knows this buyer of stolen gems. You doubtless remember that when I searched her house I found certain pieces of jewellery, which she admitted belonged to her. When I challenged her with the fact that they had been stolen, she started to say that she had been given them, but you stopped her telling me by whom. Thus a certain responsibility rests on you. For now she will not tell me who gave her that jewellery, realising that whoever it was, probably killed Denton. She wants to protect him. But what she won't tell me, she may tell you.'

'Listen,' said Tony, 'when I need a job, I'll come and ask for it. I'm not a policeman.'

'But you're a man of some courage and a little common sense,' Swanley said quietly. 'Face these facts, Mr Grey. Either Miss Mellison lied, in which case she herself is probably guilty, or she is protecting someone else, which may mean that she is only an accessory, and an unconscious and blameless one at that, never having realised that the gems were stolen, until I told her. If that is so, she is making a great mistake by trying to protect the donor. It is a mistake which might prove fatal to her, bringing the risk of being suspected of taking an active part in this series of crimes. That's a grave risk. The one way of proving her innocence, I think, is to find out who gave her the jewels. If you do what I suggest, you'll be helping her quite as much as helping us.'

He stopped. The room was quiet. Somewhere, far off, a telephone bell was ringing.

Swanley went on gently: 'Of course, if she is mixed up in it, that will hit you badly. But only a fool or a coward would refuse to take this chance of finding out the truth. Why don't you take the sensible course, Mr Grey? If you do, we may see the end of the whole business today. If you don't – ' he shrugged his shoulders.

Tony said: 'Give me a cigarette, will you?'

He took one, and lit up.

If he did what Swanley asked, he would be spying on Sarah. He couldn't do it, unless he did it in his own way. He might prove that Sarah was innocent of any crime, and safely tell Swanley what he knew. If the truth involved her, he needn't report.

Swanley said: 'I hope you'll take the sensible course, Mr Grey.'

The case had turned full circle. Tony had started with suspecting Sarah, was finishing on the same note. And – it had never been proved that she was innocent. Swanley had made that all too clear, and had made it equally clear that letting her go was a trick, to find a short cut to the truth.

Tony said abruptly: 'I'll go.'

'I'm very glad,' said Swanley, and sounded as if he meant it.

The white house and the garden, with the river just beyond, and the nearby meadows sloping down to the banks, carried that air of fictitious innocence that a mid-day sun so graciously bestows. The Daimler stood at one side, beauty and elegance on wheels. No one appeared at the windows, but as Tony reached the porch, the door opened and Sarah came out, hands extended.

'Tony, I was afraid you wouldn't come. It's wonderful to see you.'

He forced a laugh, squeezed her hands, and went in.

CHAPTER 26

Bright Idea

In his own home, dressed in flannels and a well-cut tweed jacket, Mellison looked even more imposing and arresting. He greeted Tony from the door of the drawing-room, and his handclasp was quick and firm.

'I'm glad you made it, Tony. Come in, and meet Sarah's mother.'

Mrs Mellison rose from a chair near the window, and it was obvious at a glance whence Sarah derived her good looks. Mrs Mellison was probably in the middle forties, well-preserved, with a certain magnificence that was almost regal. It wasn't until she laid her hand in Tony's, limp and lifeless, that the impression of character and regality faded.

She had a sweet, rather affected voice.

'I am so glad to meet a *valued* friend of my daughter's, Mr Grey, and you are very welcome.'

'Thank you.' It was impossible not to sound formal.

'As you know, we have just returned from Paris,' said Mrs Mellison. 'It has been a great trouble.'

'And it's all over,' Mellison said, a shade too heartily. 'What will you have to drink, my dear? Sherry?'

'Thank you, Victor.'

'Gin and orange for me,' said Sarah. She crossed to her mother's side; it was the difference between light and shade. 'You'll soon be on your way back to Paris, darling.' She patted her mother's hand.

'Whisky, Tony?' asked Mellison.

'Thanks.' The normality and friendliness of this house, coming so quickly after the talk with Swanley, made it difficult to be natural. 'I've been tippling too much lately.'

'You needed something to help you stand the strain.' Mellison poured the drinks. 'I've talked seriously to Sarah on the folly of trying to deceive the police! She was luckier than she deserved. What did Swanley have to say?'

'Oh, he was full of dark warnings to foolish young men. Apparently they've caught another crook, and have learnt that Denton was one of a gang.'

'Who killed him?' asked Sarah.

Tony shrugged. 'If Swanley knows, he hasn't confided in me. Probably a complete stranger. I wonder what would have happened if we'd all told Swanley the simple truth. from the beginning? You and I, for a start – Mrs Denton and McNaughton, even Asterley and –'

'How is McNaughton?' asked Mellison.

'Rather better, but still on the danger list, I gather.'

'It will be a *terrible* shock to Mrs McNaughton,' said Mrs Mellison unexpectedly, 'she is not a woman with whom I have much in common, but she positively *dotes* on Patrick. He is a most disturbing young man. So *aggressive*. I was always very pleased, Sarah dear, when you broke off your engagement to him.'

Mellison chuckled.

'You know Sarah's lurid reputation, I hope, Tony.'

Sarah grimaced at him.

'Everyone has such a keen imagination in the country, and red hair is rather a challenge to it!'

'Patrick McNaughton was *not* one of your more fortunate choices,' said her mother.

'Oh, I don't know.' Sarah's eyes gleamed. 'He's strong, handsome, and at least he knows what he wants.'

Tony looked at her, hurt by her beauty, unaffected by her flippancy. If he came to know her better, if the dream of marriage came true, he would have to get used to these light-hearted moods. He contrasted her now with the angry young woman on the common and at Asterley's; life with her might be enraging, but it would never be a bore.

Sarah looked back at him.

'Tony, I am going to make a confession. Upstairs in my room is a diary with the names and telephone numbers of twenty-seven young men who've dated me.'

'Sarah, I *do* wish you wouldn't use this American slang,' protested Mrs Mellison.

'It's colloquial now,' said Sarah. 'Do you disapprove, Tony?'

'Terribly! You try fixing dates with them in future, and then I'll tell you what I think about it.'

She was very young. He hadn't realised until then how young; twenty-one or two, no more, and in some curious way, unspoilt and natural. Yet Swanley had believed her guilty of murder, still wasn't sure that she was completely innocent.

'And you may as well know now that I shall take strong exception to you receiving presents from past or present admirers,' he said lightly.

'Oh, I never accept presents.'

'I should think not,' said Mrs Mellison.

'Except of course from those who were really rich or extremely good friends,' mocked Mellison.

'Daddy – '

'Really, Sarah!'

A feeling as of icy water suddenly poured into his veins assailed Tony; yet he grinned.

'Anyhow, that's settled. No presents,' he said.

'I should hope, Sarah, that if you ever accepted a valuable gift from *any* man with whom you were trifling, you would return it,' Mrs Mellison said righteously.

'I ate most of them,' said Sarah.

'Chocolates don't count.' Tony went across to the window, where he could see the sun shining on the river and, much closer, the flowers waving in glorious colour. 'You may even keep the lipsticks.' He turned, smiling, to look at her. 'The really valuable things are different.'

'Such as?'

He shrugged. 'I wouldn't know, being only a struggling

writer. Incidentally, aren't we taking rather a lot for granted?'

'Sarah always does,' Mellison said. 'Rings and watches, pearls and baubles – send them back, Sarah.'

'Father!' It was the first time she had shown any tartness. 'Anyone would think I'd been digging for gold all my life.'

'You've always *loved* jewels, and beautiful things,' said Mrs Mellison, looking at Tony thoughtfully. 'I wouldn't say you are a person with *in*expensive tastes, dear.'

'Let's change the subject,' Sarah said abruptly. 'It should be unnecessary to state yet again that I have never accepted valuable gifts. Another drink, Tony?'

'No, really, thanks.'

She went across and poured out another gin-and-orange. She didn't look at them. Her father watched her, smiling. Tony turned away. He knew she *had* accepted gifts of great value; he had heard her say so. There were two sickening facts in his mind; that she had done this, and that she was lying about it. Light-hearted and facetious, pretending great innocence, almost naïveté, he saw how she might have built up everything she had told him on a foundation of lies.

The ugliness of it contrasted hideously with her beauty.

She sipped her drink.

'Let's talk about something really interesting. You, for instance, Tony! Heavens, I hardly know a thing about you, except a few little discoveries I shall for the moment keep to myself.'

'Is writing a very *secure* profession?' asked Mrs Mellison, the innocence of her voice belied by the sharpness of her eye.

'Darling, writing is an *art*,' said Sarah. 'That's why so few authors make money. Isn't it, Tony? I – Tony!' She moved swiftly across to him. 'Darling, I've had a brainwave. Perhaps you've been writing the wrong kind of stuff. Why not write about what happened to *us*. You needn't –'

'Sarah!' cried Mrs Mellison.

'Oh, this is serious,' said Sarah, her eyes alight with enthusiasm. 'Tony, it might be exactly the right thing, your perfect medium. And what a crime story it would make! I read hundreds, I'm sure there's a fortune in them, and here's all the material for a first-rate thriller to hand!'

'Not a bad idea,' said Mellison.

Tony laughed. 'It might be worth trying, I certainly haven't found the right medium yet.'

'I could explain the true frame of mind of a person under arrest for murder,' Sarah said, thoughtfully. 'And look at the villains you have! Denton, the two men who're caught – you could make McNaughton into a kind of grey, off-black villain, too. And suspects – Anne Denton, even Dr Asterley, you yourself – Tony, you must write it.'

'I don't think the best writers write to order,' Mellison said drily. 'But you've some good background, Tony. This jewel ring, or whatever it's called, good knowledge of police methods, and what it feels like to be a suspect. It would get the whole business out of your system, too. And you'll know the villain, before long. Sarah could be a temptress of the more seductive kind.'

'I shall be the heroine,' declared Sarah. 'Tempestuous and unpredictable, but – ' she broke off. 'Oh, forget it, Tony! Anyhow, we don't know who killed Denton, yet.' She was abrupt. 'I've a feeling that it's someone in Wallingham, someone we know. I suppose it could have been Pat.'

Mellison was serious. 'Steady, old girl.'

'Why should we be steady?' demanded Sarah, and her eyes became stormy. 'We've been talking a lot of nonsense for the last half-hour, silly surface chatter. Is that so much better than a few reasonable deductions? And we *don't* know the murderer. It could have been Pat. Couldn't it?' She walked across the room, hands clasped, in deadly earnest. 'If he killed Denton, and Denton's friends wanted their revenge, they would try to kill him. Someone did. Just as they tried to kill Anne Denton, me and Tony. I won't really have a minute's peace until I know the whole truth.'

Her father made a mock cry of alarm.

'Don't look at *me*.'

'What on earth is happening in the kitchen?' asked Mrs

Mellison plaintively. 'It's after one o'clock. Those maids are impossible. I suppose I'd better go and see what's happening out there.' She sailed across the room, a vision of inanimate beauty, closing the door softly behind her.

Sarah said: 'Let's be deadly earnest for a change, and look at *facts*. Unless the police do know who killed Denton, we're still suspect. You as well as I, Tony. Father pulled some fast legal trick, I expect, and got me out, but it isn't over yet!' Her tone and her look gave challenge, as she turned abruptly to Tony. 'Did Swanley tell you something that you haven't told us?'

'Heavens no!'

'Did you know that Anne Denton thinks you were behind the shooting?'

'Sarah – ' began her father.

'Please be quiet! Tony, did you know?'

He said quietly: 'Yes. Who told you?'

'Mrs McNaughton telephoned. She gave me a dread warning against you. Be careful of that woman, she's a great hater. She always hoped that Pat and I would get married, although she pretended she didn't care a snap when we broke off our engagement. Yes, we *were* engaged, for nearly a year. Father, why are you grinning at me like that?'

Mellison said: 'I was thinking, my dear, that you seem determined to give Tony the worst possible impression.'

'I want him to know the *truth*, I want to know all the truth myself. You don't know what it's like, to have a life sentence hanging over you, to be suspected of *murder*.' Her voice was harsh, and there was a sharp catch in it. 'Could it have been Pat? Was he fooling Anne Denton? *Was* he?'

'We'll soon be able to find out,' Mellison said urbanely. 'I've asked her to come here, after luncheon. I've asked Asterley, too, and Mrs McNaughton. Between us, we might be able to find that elusive truth. Ah, there's the gong.'

CHAPTER 27

Sarah?

Mellison went out as the gong was still echoing. Sarah stood quite still, staring at the open door. Tony moved towards her, and she turned suddenly and gripped his arm, so hard that it was painful.

'Tony,' she whispered, 'I'm frightened.'

'Forget it.'

'I can't. I've been frightened from the moment I met you, on the common. Everything else has been a fake, I'm just – terrified. Who killed him? Will they blame me, or – will they blame *you*.' She shifted her grip, held his wrists tightly, and stared at him, the fire in her eyes giving them a piercing loveliness. 'Will they, Tony? I couldn't stand it. Oh, I've lived fast, but I've never been in love before. Do you understand? I've never been in love, but I love you, and I'm frightened.'

'Sarah, you needn't –'

'Tony! Words don't matter. Answer me – *did you kill Denton?*' She caught her breath again. 'I don't care if you did, he was evil, he deserved to die, I don't care if you did, I'd lie black was white to save you, but – I must know. Did you kill him?'

'No,' said Tony.

Her eyes were blazing.

'That's the truth, isn't it? Yes, I can see it's the truth, but – you found the body, and I was near. They'll try to prove that it was one of us. I've felt from the first that it would happen. Swanley didn't let me go because father's solicitor out-talked him, he had a reason. I felt that I was walking out of prison into a trap, that I was being watched all the time. I still do. I keep looking out of the window, to see if anyone's there. It wouldn't surprise me to see a detective behind a bush, to go into the back garden and find one there. I'm – terrified, Tony.'

'You must shake yourself out of it!' He gripped her arms tightly – and then suddenly she seemed to melt against him, and their lips touched, then pressed fiercely; it was as if the breath was torn out of his body.

They drew away from each other.

'No one can take *that* away,' Sarah said, with strange gentleness. 'Tony, I'm going to need you, I can feel it. I'm going to need a friend as I've never needed one in my life before.'

'There's no need to worry. I don't think Swanley suspects either of us now.'

'Don't you?' she said, and shivered.

Her mother called out, in a long-suffering tone:

'Sarah, *do* come.'

Sarah stood with her eyes closed, and Tony could see the tears trying to force themselves beneath her lids. She shook her head suddenly, fiercely, forcing a smile.

'Yes, I know I'm a fool. Coming!' She took his arm. 'Mother hates being kept waiting.'

Why should she be so frightened, unless she knew that she had cause to fear? Could anything but guilt explain that sudden outburst?

Luncheon was a form of torture. Mrs Mellison appeared to be unaware of any tension, Mellison did an urbane best to keep conversation going, Sarah plunged in occasionally, and then fell silent. It was a superbly cooked meal, which Tony hardly tasted; he wasn't hungry, didn't want to eat. His thoughts ranged over the too obvious reason for Sarah's mood, and the three people who were coming. He believed he could understand why Mellison had sent for them – in the hope of forcing the truth, believing that one of them knew it. Did Mellison know what was behind Sarah's mood now?

Coffee was served as a clock struck two.

'Now I must go and put on a sober frock worthy of the occasion,' Sarah said, jumping up five minutes later. 'A pity I haven't one embroidered with jet bugles.'

'Really, Sarah! And now, I'm sure you'll all excuse me.' Mrs Mellison rose to her feet. 'I *do* feel rather tired after the journey, and the shock. Perhaps – a little rest – '

'Of course,' said Mellison. 'We promise not to wake you.'

He shut the door after the two women and went to the sideboard, taking out a squat bottle of brandy. He moved with great ease, in his way as graceful as Sarah. He had her gift of naturalness, too, but nothing of his wife's artificiality.

After pouring out, he sat down in the chair which Sarah had left, nearer Tony.

'I wanted a few minutes quiet talk,' he said. 'I hope you know how much I appreciate the way you stood by Sarah. There's no point in emphasising it, but I shall always be grateful. There's plenty of point in trying to find out what's worrying her. Do you know?'

'Fear that she'll be accused again,' Tony suggested.

'Oh, it's not that. You don't know Sarah well enough. Danger to herself doesn't mean anything to her. She may feel fear but never submit to it. She's submitting to this – I've never known her so nervy. Sure you don't know why?'

Tony said slowly: 'You want the blunt truth?'

'I'd expect nothing else from you.'

'Then there's one way her fear could be explained; if she did it.' The words came out abruptly, while Mellison watched him closely, showing no sense of surprise or shock.

'I suppose that's true. Haven't you thought beyond that?'

'I don't see anything beyond it,' Tony said, 'and I'm as worried as hell.'

'Really fond of her?'

'Fond!'

Mellison smiled.

'If ever anyone asked for trouble, it was Sarah. But I

always felt that frivolity was a phase she would outgrow, and that she would have the sense to fall in love with someone of worth and integrity in the end. I'm glad that you met in the way you did, and I hope all goes well. You don't need telling that nothing will be plain sailing, with Sarah, but if she wants a thing enough, she'll do anything to get it – and if she loves enough, she'll do anything to bring happiness. You'd be surprised if you knew what sacrifices she's made, one way and another, for me and for her mother.' Mellison stood up abruptly, and didn't enlarge on that cryptic statement. 'I'll be down again in ten minutes or so, the others aren't due until a quarter to three.'

Tony said: 'Do you know why she's frightened?'

'I've a good idea,' said Mellison, and went out without another word.

Mrs McNaughton was sullen, Anne Denton pale and shocked, only half in this world. Asterley had little to say, obviously as puzzled as Tony about Mellison's reason for bringing them together. Sarah did a brittle best to keep conversation going.

Tony was next to Asterley for a few seconds.

'What is all this?'

'Victor Mellison didn't plan this get-together for nothing,' said Asterley. 'He's trying to find out who's most liable to crack.'

'Why should any of them crack?'

Asterley shrugged.

Mellison said amiably: 'We aren't getting much further, are we?'

'I'm going home,' declared Mrs McNaughton. 'I can't stay in this man's company any longer.' She glared at Tony.

Mellison smiled.

'Why hate Tony? Why not hate the real villains of the piece?' His tone was faintly mocking. 'Mrs Denton, you've known Pat McNaughton for months. I know – I've seen you together, in London.'

There was a hush; broken when Mrs McNaughton drew in a hissing breath.

'Haven't you?' Mellison asked.

Anne gasped: 'No, it's a lie!'

'Oh, but it isn't. Why did you kill Denton?'

'I didn't kill him! I was in love with him, I –'

'When I tell the police about your old acquaintance, what do you think they'll say?'

Anne didn't speak.

Sarah took Tony's hand.

Mrs McNaughton cried: 'Anne!'

Anne Denton jumped up, looked towards the door, as if seeking a way of escape. She was trembling violently.

'Did – you – know – Pat?' demanded Mrs McNaughton.

'I –'

'Did you?'

Anne cried: 'Yes, yes, I did, but I didn't kill anyone! And you needn't be so angry – your precious Pat was in it! He's bought and sold stolen jewels for years, he worked with Ray. I tell you he did!'

She burst into tears, talking on and on...

She had lied; she had known that Denton had the stolen jewels and the notebook. Denton had stolen that from his own boss, wanted to work the gang by himself. Pat McNaughton was deeply involved.

She had known that Denton's leader would try to get them back, and believed Tony had stolen them. She had lied about the message appearing to come from Tony; she'd known who it was from, she and McNaughton had gone to the Inn, to try to come to terms – and hadn't reckoned on the shooting.

They hadn't the jewels or the notebook.

Anne swore she had not killed Denton – and it was difficult not to believe her.

The police took her away, and Asterley, with tact and

kindness, withdrew with Mrs McNaughton.

Sarah and Tony, in the drawing-room, watched them go off. Mellison came in from the porch and closed the front door, but didn't enter the drawing-room. They heard him walking upstairs, and a few minutes afterwards, caught a murmur of voices which was cut off when a door closed. Sarah went quickly across the room and closed this door. She was pale, now that the tension of the meeting was over, and her eyes looked heavy. There was no doubt of the weight of fear still upon her.

'Sarah, why are you so frightened?' Tony's voice was taut.

'I can't – help myself.'

Sooner or later, he would have to tell her what he thought; that the only real cause was knowledge of her guilt. At the back of his mind was Swanley's request; he'd fought against asking her point-blank, but the moment was approaching when it couldn't be put off any longer. As he watched her, it seemed as if he had known her all his life; everything about her was dear and precious. And he sensed that she felt the same about him. It was an indefinable conviction, that they were right for each other; and between them stood the shadow of murder, and of her fear, and of her knowledge of the truth.

For he was sure that she knew.

She went across to the piano, and began to play a light and lively piece, one entirely out of accord with the moment. He watched her hands, her long, sensitive fingers. She wore one diamond ring. He wondered, with a sudden constriction of his heart, whether it was the engagement ring that McNaughton had given her.

She stopped abruptly.

'Sarah,' Tony said, and leaned against the piano, looking down at her.

'Let's not talk,' she said nervously.

'We must talk. You know who killed Denton, don't you?'

She flared up. 'No! What a foul thing to say!'

'All the same, you know.'

'Are you accusing me again?'

'I'm not accusing – '

'Of course you are!' she flashed at him. 'You did when we were on the common. It was obvious then that you thought I'd killed him. Well, I didn't! And you talk about being in love, how can you love me, if you think I killed him?'

Her cheeks were flushed, now, and her eyes held that familiar angry brilliance; but she did not strike a responding chord of anger in him, and his voice was quite steady.

'Listen to me, Sarah. I am not accusing you, but I am sure you know the whole truth. That's what is frightening you. But if I thought you'd killed him – if I knew you'd killed him – it wouldn't stop me from loving you. Does that make sense?'

'No!'

'Well, it's true. Sarah – '

'How can you stand there and talk like this? If this is all you can do, I don't want you here. Understand that.'

'Sarah, losing your temper isn't going to help, unless towards a life sentence.'

She jumped up, her hands raised.

'I didn't kill him, they can't convict me!'

'It could happen, if you – '

'Don't talk like that!' Her voice was hoarse with rage, he had never seen her so angry; and he knew that she wasn't acting, this was exactly how she felt, possessed by a tempestuous fury. She would strike out, to hurt, to wound, without caring whom she attacked. She clutched her throat, and her fingers bit into the creamy whiteness. 'Do you understand what you're saying? That day after day after day I will be enclosed within stone walls, never to lie in the sun, or touch flowers, never to walk alone down a white road. That's what you're saying – and you'll help them, you'll believe that I could have done it. Get away from me. Get away. I hate the sight of you!'

He was still calm.

'You know, just what it will mean, so why take the risk. Who gave you those stolen jewels, Sarah?'

'Get out of my sight!'

'Losing your temper just won't help. Either someone gave them to you and you're fighting to save them, or else you lied to Swanley, and knew they were stolen. What's the truth, Sarah?'

'Will – you – leave – this – house?'

'Not yet. Where did you get them?'

She flew at him, and he had to grapple with her, much as he had grappled with Mrs McNaughton. There was the strength of fury in her, and he backed away under the fierceness of her onslaught, but at last caught her wrists and held them tight, pressed them against her breast. She glared at him, and never had she looked more beautiful.

'Where did you get those jewels, Sarah?'

'Get out of this house!'

'Did someone give them to you, or did you lie to Swanley? Let me have the truth.'

She tried to struggle again, but he held her fast.

'Get away from me,' she sobbed, 'I hate the sight of you. Get away!'

'Who gave them to you? Who do you want to save? Who is worth imprisonment, Sarah? Whether they incarcerate you or whether they don't, depends on who you got those jewels from. You know it, that's what is making you behave so wildly. You're defending someone – *who*, Sarah?'

She didn't answer this time, but stood staring into his eyes, still breathing heavily.

'Tell me,' he said gently. 'Whatever you've done, I love you, nothing can make any difference to that. If you killed Denton, then I'd rather die myself than let you be hurt, but if it's someone else –'

She collapsed against him, suddenly, and began to cry; not noisily, but with the hopeless misery of despair. He put his arms round her comfortingly, seeing that the door was open, but not remembering that she had closed it. Her sobs racked her body, and he felt tautness at his throat and a prickling heat at his eyes.

Gradually, she quietened.

'Sarah,' he said, 'everything depends on the truth about those jewels. Who gave them to you?'

She didn't answer, but stirred in his arms, and looked up at him. Her cheeks were smeared with tears and her eyes were heavy; she was not beautiful, now. She was helpless and miserable, and because he did not know the truth, he was as frightened for her.

'You must tell me,' he persisted. 'We'll never get free, unless you tell me. It'll blast our whole future. Sarah we won't have a chance. Where did you get the jewels? Who gave them to you?'

She buried her face against his breast, and uttered a name that he didn't hear.

'What was that?' His own voice was so low that he doubted whether she had heard. 'Sarah – '

She drew back from him, and there was despair on her face, touched with horror and with dread.

She said clearly: 'My father.'

CHAPTER 28

Simple Truth

'My father,' she repeated, and shuddered. 'Tony, it's true. You mustn't tell anyone, you mustn't tell Swanley. But he gave them to me.' Her voice was hoarse. 'When Swanley asked me, I realised the truth. I've feared it for a long time. Yes, father gave them to me, and – '

'But he was in Paris!'

'He wasn't,' said Sarah. 'He took mother over there and left her for a day, flew back to London and came down here, then flew back to Paris the same evening. I saw him. He was disguised, but I knew who it was. I saw him after lunch, on the day Denton was killed. He knew all about it; that's how he knew about Anne and McNaughton.'

Silence fell.

This, then, was the truth. Tony, accepting what she said, could now understand everything. He could understand her horror, too.

'What shall I *do*?' she whispered.

The door opened wider, and Mellison came in.

He smiled as he walked across to Sarah, and put a hand on her hair, as if she were a little child. She looked at him, with her eyes brimming with tears. His smile broadened and yet he was very gentle.

'I wondered if you knew,' he said.

'Why – why did you do it?' she whispered.

'Partly for your sake, but perhaps mostly for my own,' said Mellison, calmly. 'I've been operating a jewel gang with Denton and others for years, and I've run a currency ring, giving the authorities plenty of trouble. I've lived by crime for a long time, my dear – and I hoped you'd never know.'

'Denton,' said Sarah, chokily. 'You – '

'Yes, I killed him. He stole my list of contacts, wanted to take over from me, squeezing me out. Then I discovered that he was blackmailing you. I talked to him in London before flying to Paris. He boasted about his influence over you, said he was seeing you next day.

'So I took your mother to Paris, left her there, and came back.

'I followed you.

'Remember, you went to the theatre club first, to deliver a letter. The door was open and I followed you in, thinking that I would stop you from going. You went out by a side door. While I was there, I saw a baseball bat – one had been brought down from the stage.'

Sarah's hand crept into Tony's; her fingers were cold.

'I slipped one under my jacket and went back to the car I'd hired for the trip. I wore a beard and moustache,' Mellison went on, 'and no casual acquaintance would have recognised me. Then I went to the common. Denton had told me where he was to meet you – near the end of the trenches. So I hid in them, until he arrived – alone. He didn't see or hear me approach. We must have all the truth now; I meant to kill him – because of what he was doing to you, as well as what he'd tried to do to me. I think he died with the first blow.

'I took the diamonds and the notebook out of his pocket, then walked back along the trenches, and saw you both arrive. You went off, Sarah, Anne Denton came along, and Tony left her alone there. I hurried off, without being seen. I drove back to London, and was in Paris again that night.

'I hoped, and believed, that it would be left as an unsolved crime, but realised you might be in acute danger. When I knew you were, I came back. Then I discovered what was happening. Denton, his so-called wife and McNaughton had plotted against me, and they used Hollen and another man, both clever cracksmen. With Denton dead, McNaughton and the woman wanted the jewels and the book. Hollen and his colleague also wanted them. Hollen was behind the attacks on you, then quarrelled with McNaughton. Hollen thought McNaughton was double-crossing. Then I discovered the whole story.

'Denton and his wife – I'm sorry for her, she was in love with him – had plotted with McNaughton to squeeze me out. Denton brought Hollen and another clever jewel thief into it, but after Denton was killed, Hollen saw himself as the big shot. Hollen knew Denton had a contact man here, but didn't know it was McNaughton. He thought at first it was you.

'He discovered it was McNaughton.

'He fixed the meeting at the Corner Inn – and Mrs Denton must have been so frightened, afterwards, that to try to keep McNaughton out of more trouble, she involved you, Tony. Hollen told the police a plausible mixture of the truth and lies – he'd gone there to frighten McNaughton into handing over the goods – which I had.

'That's the story, my darling.' Mellison paused, still smiling faintly. 'I let you suffer hell, trying to save myself, but it didn't work. When the others have told everything. the police will get on to me.'

He stopped, and took his hand from her shoulder.

'Now it's all over,' he said. 'I'm sorry that you had to stand the strain, sorry that you'll have to grieve, but – there's Tony. He'll look after you better than I could.' He paused. 'There's just one other thing, my dear – about your mother. It will be a great shock to her, but won't go deep. She'll want to move away from here, and I should let her. Get married, as soon as you can, and – *don't* live with your mother. Goodbye, now.'

He moved away.

Sarah cried: 'Daddy! Daddy, what are you going to do?'

'I'm going to see Swanley, of course,' Mellison said. 'Isn't that the obvious thing? I'm going to give him that notebook!'

He turned and hurried away, while Sarah huddled, quivering, against Tony. They watched the Daimler turn out of the drive gates.

Sarah said in a quavering voice: 'I've been afraid of something like this. Denton hinted at it, that was why I paid him blackmail. I couldn't tell you before, I –'

She broke off.

The first Swanley heard of it was a report from a village constable, fifteen miles out of Wallingham. A Daimler car, driven at terrific speed, had smashed into a brick wall, and the driver had been killed instantaneously. The policeman had telephoned Wallingham, because the driver was Victor Mellison.

Swanley went to the scene, found Mellison – and the notebook in his pocket.

When Swanley reached the white house, Tony and Sarah had found the confession note, addressed to the Superintendent, on Mellison's dressing-table.

Jameson was the first reporter to find out the truth.

It was two months before Tony found a buyer for the house in Middle Street, and moved to London. Sarah and her mother already had a small flat in Kensington, and he rented some unfurnished rooms nearby. Mellison had been right in his judgement of his wife's reaction. She was already nearly her old self, and was making life a round of bridge parties and petty interests.

Tony's rooms, large and airy, were on the third floor of a terrace house. He furnished them with some pieces from Middle Street, and a few others that Sarah had brought from the house by the river. He was alone one evening during his first week there, when there was a knock on the door. He expected Sarah.

Asterley beamed at him, when he opened it.

'Hallo, Rick! Come in.' Tony stood on one side. 'Is Dora with you?'

'No, not this time.' Asterley looked round. 'Not bad at all, Tony. For one or for two?'

'Two eventually.'

'Soon, I hope,' said Asterley, dropping into an easy chair. 'Well, things have settled down in Wallingham. Mrs McNaughton's dropped out of everything, but such energy and bossiness can't be damped down for ever, and soon, I hope, there will be a resurge of it. Has Swanley told you about that diamond you had as a gift?'

'No.'

'From McNaughton. He had the jewel, was afraid his house would be searched, and got rid of it by posting it to you through a friend in London. The idea was to make the police suspect you as the Wallingham contact man. Mrs Denton tried it on again, later.'

'I don't know how he thought the diamond would involve me,' said Tony.

'That's due to your innocence! You might have held on to it – and if the police had searched and found it, you'd have been in Queer Street. McNaughton couldn't conceive of simple honesty like yours. He was desperate, of course – like Hollen, who sent the note to Sarah. Hollen thought you were the contact man – and as you were so friendly with Sarah, she must be in it. How is Sarah?'

'Fine!'

'Recovering?'

'Slowly. She'll be all right,' Tony said. 'It'll always haunt her, but – well, that'll get less and less.'

'Quarrel much?' Asterley asked, with a crooked grin.

'Not yet!'

'When you start, she'll really have got over being haunted,' Asterley said. 'You probably think you're a lucky man, but I think she's a fortunate young woman. Ever thought of writing that book, by the way? She mentioned it to me.'

'It's nearly finished,' said Tony. 'I'm a bit shaken by my own part – I just stood back and let things happen to me. Sarah's reading it now, I'm expecting her –'

The front door bell rang. Tony's face lit up, and he hurried to open it.

Sarah burst in, without a greeting, flushed, excited.

'Tony, you're impossible! I've just read the bit where I was at Rick Asterley's place. I couldn't have behaved like that. To think that you put such a construction on what I said – oh!' She broke off. 'Rick!'

'I'm not worried about you any longer,' Asterley said, standing up lazily. 'You're right back in form. Don't let her get away with anything, Tony – be firm. By the way – Swanley sends his regards.'

THE END

LAY HER AMONG THE LILIES by JAMES HADLEY CHASE

It was odd that a healthy young heiress like Janet Crosby should die of heart failure. Odder still, that on the day she died she sent a note and $500 to Vic Malloy, private investigator, asking him to trace the person who was blackmailing her sister.

Intrigued by the note, Malloy tried to see Maureen Crosby but only got as far as her nurse – a curvaceous blonde with an engaging bedside manner. Next he tried to see Janet's personal maid, but found that somebody else had reached her first and made sure that she wouldn't talk to anyone – ever again . . .

552 09551 6 – 40p T170

I WOULD RATHER STAY POOR by JAMES HADLEY CHASE

Like most bank managers, Dave Calvin had acquired an irresistible charm that he could switch on whenever he felt the necessity. Underneath it he was cold, calculating, brutal – a perfect murderer . . .

For years he waited – watching an endless stream of money pass through his hands – knowing that a risk was only worth taking if the reward was justified. And a three hundred thousand dollar payroll was justification enough – even for murder . . .

552 09491 9 – 40p T171

THE LAST COP OUT by MICKEY SPILLANE

Gillian Burke–known as Gill – had been the toughest, biggest and most effective cop in New York. That was until the Mob decided he was getting too dangerous and pulled the strings which got him dishonourably removed from the force.

But – even disgraced – Gill was still the only cop who knew how the Mob operated, and when their top operators began to be put violently out of business Gill was persuaded – by a frightened district attorney– to put his badge back on and find the killer.

His investigation had hardly begun when he became involved with a cop's daughter – Helen – who was on the syndicate's payroll, and Helga, a luscious Swedish blonde who made her living out of love. But even with such delightful diversions Gill found himself trapped in one of the bloodiest vendettas of all time, pitted against a faceless assassin whose sole aim was destruction. . . .

0 552 09577 X – 45p T193

THE ERECTION SET by MICKEY SPILLANE

Dogeron Kelly, a walking bomb of a man, suddenly appears in elegant– and not so elegant – New York circles with a suitcase containing a quarter of a million dollars. There are rumours, but no-one is certain where he, or the money, came from. It seems he is out to claim his inheritance– or is there something else he is after?

Sharon Cass, for instance, a bright and beautiful girl with some very special gifts for the right man?

Whatever it is, Dog Kelly isn't telling, but his search takes in a baronial old-family manor; the high levels of international illegal traffic; paid mobsters; the rich and the famous . . .

THE ERECTION SET

Another blockbuster by one of the world's most popular writers.

0 552 09111 1 – 40p T74